Hell's Butcher

Book Two in the Hell's Butcher Series

Chris Barili

Hell's Butcher

Formatting by Rik - Wild Seas Formatting
(http://www.WildSeasFormatting.com)
Cover art by Michelle Johnson of Blue Sky Design
Edited by Jennifer Severino

Printed in the United States of America

ACKNOWLEDGMENTS

Thanks to Jennifer Severino from Twitching Pen Editing, Rik Hall of Wild Seas Formatting (formatting), and Michelle Johnson of Blue Sky Designs (cover art). You guys made this book better than I ever could have without you.

DEDICATION

This one is for you, M. You made sure I wasn't alone in the dark, then led me out of it. I can never repay your friendship and love, nor will I ever deserve either. But I will always treasure them, for they alone have sustained me. {{{{{{{{{{M}}}}}}}}}}

CHAPTER ONE

Frank sat bolt upright, his forehead hitting a padded surface in front of him, making lights dance before his eyes. He lay back down, his head finding a soft pillow beneath it, and he opened his eyes.

Total darkness.

He listened. The clackity-clack and swaying told him he was on a moving train.

"Where the Sam Hell?"

His hands found the surface in front of him: padded velvet, with cool brass rivets holding it in place. Almost like…

He shoved, and the lid lifted, allowing a dim light to stream in as he sat up and found himself in a coffin, its lacquered sides gleaming in the dusty light. Cold air washed across his face. Not just cold—frigid, crackling cold, like the air itself might snap at the slightest pressure. The light came from a sliding door on his right, cracked just enough to admit a shaft of yellow sun.

He rubbed his eyes and fought to erase the images of the dream from his mind, but they were barbed, like porcupine quills, and hurt to try and rip them out.

He'd stood on a rocky outcropping that overlooked a valley swarming with men locked in mortal combat. One side wore blue, the other gray, and they killed one another with efficiency and zeal. Men screamed as bullets tore through them, or died silently, impaled on blades. Cannons fired, rockets burst overhead, and so much blood flowed that the ground turned to an ocean of red and the sky became a filthy crimson reflection of the death below.

Something rose on the horizon, a shape so huge, it blotted out the sun. Tufts of thick hair dotted obsidian skin, muscles rippling. Clawed hands reached out across the scene, spreading more death. Black strings stretched from its fingertips to each man on the battlefield, the immense puppeteer somehow controlling everything at once, his fingers turning to blurs.

As men died, the creature grew. The warped features of its face curved into a grim smile as it took in the death it had caused and found it satisfying. Eyes glowing redder than the sky scanned the carnage, then locked onto Frank and turned black as night.

One hand reached for him, puppet strings snapping at him like snakes. Frank turned to run, but the blood congealed around his ankles and locked him in place, his feet making slurping sounds as he fought to pull free. The hand swept down, and cold, biting cords wrapped around him, squeezing like steel cables.

The next thing he knew, Frank had his gun out, firing indiscriminately into the mass of writhing bodies. Every snap of the strings made him shoot. He dropped rebel and union alike, killing for the sake of doing so, not even taking aim. Men died by his hand in droves, falling in agony.

Frank tried to stop, but the strings kept twitching, and every time they did, he fired again. And again and again.

The train shuddered, jarring Frank from the memory. Two more caskets sat beside him, and as he watched, their lids opened. Spike sat up in one, and Camille rose from the other, both rubbing their eyes.

The three exchanged a glance, and Frank hurried to open the door and peer outside.

Right away, he wished he hadn't.

The tracks ahead of them stretched for another mile or so, lines reaching off toward the horizon. Ties and ballast zipped past under the train, blurs of night against the orange ground. At the end of the tracks stood a trestle bridge, its brown spires like spider legs holding a long-dead insect as an offering. The bridge curved right across a deep, shadowed gorge before disappearing into the tiny hole of a tunnel on the far side.

Halfway across, just before the curve, flames engulfed the span, devouring the wooden supports and ties.

"Aw, Hell," Frank muttered.

Camille joined him at the door, staring ahead at their impending doom, blue eyes calm and cool as ice.

Flames roared ahead of them, and the bridge gave a loud, moaning crack. The fire blazed all the way to the tunnel now, and as it consumed the trestle supports, the bridge swayed.

A section of it fell away on the far side of the curve, leaving a gap of about twenty yards, an impossible distance for a heavy, laden train engine. Frank watched chunks of the bridge disappear into the impossible blackness of the gorge, and fought the urge to throw up.

"It's not real," she told him. "Just like the coach, this is just the underworld's way of getting you across the barrier and into the living world."

Spike joined them, swallowing hard as they sped toward the collapsed section.

"I wish the underworld could be less dramatic."

The train picked up speed, barreling onto the shaky bridge, leaning to the left and nearly derailing through the turn. But the demonic engineer blew the whistle, its deathly call echoing through the canyon, and somehow righted the train. Their car slammed back down on the rails, nearly tossing Frank and his friends from the doorway.

They streaked toward the fallen span. Twenty yards. Ten. Five.

Frank's stomach lurched as the engine leapt the gap, hauling its line of cars behind it. The engine and the first two cars landed safely on the other side, but not theirs. It fell just short, front wheels on the track, but the rest of the car dangling over the edge.

The car jerked backwards as the weight of the rest of the train tumbled off the bridge, still coupled. Frank looked back to see the bridge behind them collapse into the chasm, the long snake of cars dangling from the rear hitch of their boxcar.

"Hold on!" Frank shoved Camille back against the coffin, away from the door.

For a moment, they hung, suspended between the swaying rear end of the train and the straining, roaring engine. The whistle howled again, and sparks flew from the engine's iron wheels as it struggled against the weight, but it wasn't strong enough. They edged back with a jerk, then stopped.

"We ain't gonna make it!" cried Spike.

Behind them, the remaining cars wagged right and left, like a dog's tail. It gave Frank an idea.

"Stay here!"

He sat in the center of the car and let himself slide toward the back, bracing his feet on either side of the rear door. He opened the door to the left and tried to reach the coupler. If he could unfasten it, the rest of the cars would fall and the engineer could pull Frank and his friends up.

But his arms weren't long enough. Even with his knees bent, he couldn't reach the peg holding the knuckles together.

Then Spike was there, one massive hand on Frank's shoulder, the other holding a chain fastened to the wall.

"Give me your ankles."

Frank hesitated.

"Do it, gunfighter! You know I can hold ya!"

They slipped backward again, and the engine wailed. With a sigh, Frank nodded. He lay on his belly, with Spike holding his ankles, and slithered down until his chest hung out of the door. Below him, shadows loomed, the cars creaking and swaying above them.

Frank yanked the pin, the cars uncoupled, and the rear of the train fell away, disappearing below.

Then, their car leapt forward, nearly tossing him out the door. Had Spike not held tight, Frank would have followed the disappearing freight cars. Instead, the barkeep pulled him in, and Frank slammed the door closed as the car leveled out, safe on the tracks.

He lay, panting, when Camille yelled.

"Don't breathe easy yet, boys!"

When he looked ahead out the side door, Frank's heart fell.

They sped, out of control, toward the tunnel, just a hundred yards ahead. The tunnel that was now blocked by a landslide of boulders.

He watched as the engineer looked back at him, tipped his hat, and laughed.

Frank closed his eyes and squeezed Camille's shoulder.

* * *

Frank awoke to the muffled, rhythmic clackity-clack of a train, and the lulling, almost wavy motion of a rail car moving down the tracks. He lay, eyes closed, and took in his surroundings through his other senses. His back pressed into something soft, like a mattress or cushion, and his hands were folded across his chest. The sound of the train reached him as if through a snowbank, soft and distant. Cool air brushed over his face, but his breath bounced back on his lips like a warm breeze.

Suddenly, he felt trapped, locked in a tiny cell with walls closing in from either side, and a ceiling pressing down, all threatening to crush him.

He opened his eyes, lunging up in the pitch black surrounding him. With a hollow thump, his head hit a cushioned surface, bouncing back to its pillow. Instinctively, his hands leapt up from his chest and shoved, knocking open a lid and allowing light to spill in as he sat up for good this time.

He found himself in a casket, again, the red velvet lining like blood in bright light of morning. Frank heaved himself out of the offensive box, his boots pounding the floorboards of another freight car. Dizziness washed over him, and he had to grasp the open lid of the casket to hold himself half-upright. He closed his eyes and waited for the vertigo to pass, then straightened and looked around.

The light spilled in from a half-open side door, a brilliant slash so bright, he couldn't actually see outside to know what it looked like. Two other caskets sat on the floor near his, their lids closed, brown stained wood shining. Frank walked to the closest one and lifted the lid. Camille blinked and shielded her eyes with a forearm, reaching for Frank with the other. He helped her to her feet, ignoring the layer of dead and rotting skin that sloughed off one of her fingers when he did.

He studied her as the blade of light fell across her face, disappointed to see blue veins running under pale, gray skin, and blueish circles under each eye.

She wore the same drab men's clothing as always, wrinkled and tattered, and her Bowie rode at her waist. A Winchester sat in the casket where she'd been.

Frank reached down absently and found the reassuring bulk of his Colt under his duster. His mind flashed back to the underworld, to Buzzy's lab, when Frank first saw the gun.

"I hesitate to give you this, Marshal," Buzzy had told him, "given your particular...work method. This is as dangerous to you as it is to the people you're after. But it isn't my place to help you face yourself. It's my job to help you bring back John Wilkes Booth and his loonies. So, here you go."

Frank had hefted the perfectly-wrought weapon, feeling its impeccable balance and ice-cold metal.

"It'll fire more lead than any normal gun could shoot

in a lifetime." Buzzy looked uncertain, shifting his weight on his feet. "Assuming you let it. All you have to do is think about what kind of bullet to use–regular, Holy Water, or green—and that's what the gun will fire. There's a bit of the Boss-man's heart in this one, I think. And thus, it has a mind of its own."

Frank saw the danger now, and suddenly felt like he'd just shoved a Satan's Scorpion into his gun belt, something that would bite deep and inject him with death.

"I see what you mean," Frank said. "If I let things get out of hand, I could kill more people. Too many people. I could kill people…"

"Forever. Without stopping." Buzzy turned his back, hands clasped behind him. "That would be worse for you than almost anything."

Back in the train, Frank shook himself and adjusted his hat on his head, just to be sure it was there.

"You look like Hell." Camille eased back and looked at his face. Her words froze in the air before her, and for the first time, Frank noticed it was cold. Really cold.

"Well, somehow, that seems appropriate," he told her, forcing himself to smile.

She shrugged and moved to the door while Frank opened the second casket. Inside, Spike snored almost as loud as the train, his hands crossed on his stomach. The Winchester laid beside him, and his bartender's apron was just as stained as before, only with a few more blood spots this time.

Frank gave his shoulder a shake, and the big man sat up, brown eyes blinking open.

"Where are we?"

Frank decided to find out, so he went to the door and stood by Camille.

Within a foot of the door, cold air buffeted him, chilling his nose and making him tug his duster tight around his shoulders. Outside, a rolling countryside coated in white rushed by, snowflakes whipping past like bullets. Trees stood bare like skeleton hands reaching up to grab the clouds, with long-needled pine trees between them the only sign of life along the tracks.

For a moment, his mind wandered back, falling into a memory of his underworld battle for redemption. It had been frozen during one of his tests there, too. When he'd faced Lisa, the woman with whom he'd made a child. The woman he'd beaten and abandoned.

Camille didn't look at him, but kept her eyes on the frozen scene along the tracks.

"It's beautiful." she shivered. "But so cold. I've never been anywhere this cold."

"Any idea where we are?"

"We just passed a sign that said Albany in 200 miles."

"We're heading east, based on the sun," he mused, scratching his chin. His fingers didn't want to move, but he forced them to. "So, we're just east of Buffalo. Should have a few hours for our bodies to rebuild, then. That's good. We need it."

She shot him a sidelong glare, but he shrugged it off.

"We're supposed to be going to Dover, New Hampshire," he went on. "I don't know how far it is from Albany to Dover, but hopefully we'll be nice and —"

Something growled.

Camille locked eyes with him, her hand falling to the handle of her knife. A wisp of green light leaked out of the scabbard, proof that Buzzy had modified her blade to deal with Hell's escapees.

"Since you seem fond of blades over bullets," Buzzy

had told her, "I thought this might be an appropriate weapon for you. The glow is a watered-down version of the green bullet Frank used to dispatch your prospector friend last time you went back. One prick with this blade will render an escaped soul helpless. A full-fledged cut or stab will send them screaming back to Hell like a banshee with their hair on fire."

Spike lifted his rifle out of the casket and looked around the interior of the car. Inside, Frank knew Spike had loaded the new Holy Water bullets Buzzy had made for the bartender.

When Spike had complained that his own Holy Water bullets hadn't killed anything, Buzzy had grinned.

"These bullets have a bit more punch. Each one is silver, and has pure Holy Water in the tip. About twice the amount you were able to put in yours, too. I even managed to get someone from up there to bless them. Hit your target in the heart with one of these, and you'll send whatever soul has possessed them right back to the pit of fire itself."

Spike nodded, a grin cracking his rocky face. "And if I hit them somewhere else?"

"It ought to knock even the toughest Hellhound right on its back."

The barkeep had grinned from ear to ear.

Frank closed his eyes and listened.

The growl came again, louder this time, and to his right. He wheeled, peering into the shadows at the back of the car. At first, he didn't see anything, but as his eyes adjusted from the bright exterior to the dim shadows before him, that changed.

Eyes reflected back the cold, morning sunlight, gold disks tracking his every movement. Below them, white fangs glistened as the creature growled again.

"How'd a damned Hellhound find us already?" Spike stepped forward, raising his gun, but Frank put his hand on the barrel and eased it down.

"That ain't no Hellhound."

He took a hesitant step toward the eyes, finding it difficult to move. His limbs had stiffened and hardened, as if they were made of wood, and it took a mountain of effort to take even one step. He did, though, and then another. In return, an even louder growl clawed its way out of the darkness. The eyes locked on him as the creature paced.

As he neared, he made out the bars of a cage, its top as high as his chest, the door secured with a massive padlock. Inside, Batcho paced back and forth, teeth bared, ears back, hackles up.

"What the Hell's your problem?" Frank snarled back at the coyote.

At the sound of Frank's voice, Batcho stopped his pacing, tilting his head to one side. His normal collar of Indian beads looked tight around his neck, as if the coyote had grown since the last time they'd met.

Camille and Spike joined Frank, one behind each of his shoulders. Batcho sniffed the air, and after a moment, he jumped back in the cage and resumed his growling.

"He wants to kill us," Spike said. "There's hate in those eyes."

Camille shook her head and stepped forward. She knelt a few feet from the cage, making Batcho snarl and snap at her behind the bars.

"No, not hate. Fear. He's scared of us."

Again, Batcho's aggressiveness flagged, as if he knew who she was. She reached out her hand, putting it just an inch from the bars. Batcho took one sniff and lunged at her, teeth flashing a ghostly green.

"Remember what Buzzy told us?" Camille rose and backed away from the cage. "He changed Batcho. Gave him a bite that'll send our escapees back to Hell, and made it so he can smell people in...our condition. And he made it a threat, in his mind. So, as far as Batcho's nose is concerned, we're dangerous."

Frank looked closer and saw the same green glow in the coyote's teeth that surrounded the special bullets that wiped souls from existence. Only this had been diluted, to only send them back to Hell. "Makes sense. That's why, when he hears our voices, he calms down. For an instant, his hearing overrules his nose."

Spike patted the rifle like he held a cat. "That's all well and good, but I think I'll keep this handy, just in case."

Frank nodded, and the three of them wandered away from the cage, back to where their caskets sat in a row. Frank looked down into his and noticed a piece of paper folded on the red velvet cushion.

He picked it up and opened it, his cold-stiffened fingers barely working. A man's chicken-scratch handwriting covered the page.

Frank and all,

Sorry for the coffins, but we needed a way to get your bodies to New Hampshire, so I faked letters saying we were re-burying you all in family plots there.

Get off the train in Albany. We will meet you there and take you to Dover.

Yours,

Stan and Curtis

"Looks like Stan's been busy." Camille's teeth chattered as she talked.

Frank put his arm around her, the stiff muscles fighting him every inch of the way, and pulled her close.

"Spike, close that door," he said. "We need to get warm in here. Our dead bodies aren't going to move well in this cold until we get rebuilt a bit more, I suspect."

Spike moved like a piece of frozen beef, but managed to roll the heavy door closed.

"Now what?" he asked. "It's still cold as, well Hell, in here."

Frank guided Camille back to her casket and eased her down onto the soft cushions. Odd that people thought the dead needed comfortable beds for their final sleep, but he was glad now that they did.

"This might be our only way," he said. "If we get back in these damned boxes and close the lids, our body heat should warm us up. And we can rebuild while we sleep."

Spike nodded and put a shivering hand on the lid of his casket as he lay down in it. "I hope you're right. Fighting Booth and his crew's gonna be real hard if they can move but we're frozen stiff."

He pulled the lid down on himself.

Frank took one last look around the car, then lay back down and closed his own lid.

He closed his eyes, but his mind wouldn't stop working. Their mission this time was different than the last. Instead of returning one escaped soul to Hell, Frank and his posse had to return six, a gang led by former presidential assassin John Wilkes Booth. He and five of his co-conspirators—George Atzerodt, Mary Surrat, David Herold, and Lewis Powell—had returned to the world of the living, and Frank had the feeling the judges hadn't been altogether honest in what they thought Booth was after.

The judges—especially Frank's old enemy Webber—believed Booth had returned to claim Booth's old flame,

Lucy Hale. They'd been secretly engaged when the actor had killed President Lincoln, and the judges seemed to think Booth wanted her back.

Frank had his doubts. Besides the fact that the judges rarely told the whole truth, it didn't seem likely someone like Booth would return for an old flame, especially not with his entire gang.

And when Frank had mentioned the security problem in Hell, the judges had shut him down in a heartbeat.

And then, there was the dream.

Something didn't add up.

Eventually, Frank fell asleep, hoping the dream didn't return.

CHAPTER TWO

He awoke when the train jerked to a stop again, alert in an instant. He flexed his arms and found they moved better now. The air inside the casket had warmed considerably, and his breath no longer froze the moment it left his mouth.

He longed to stay still, to rest until someone re-buried the casket and he could just stay there indefinitely. But he knew what would happen then. His mind would wander to thoughts of Ron and Lisa, to the people he'd wronged in life. His guilt would swell up like a boil needing lanced, until it hurt so badly, he'd long for a return to Hell, where agony was more manageable.

So, with a sigh, he pushed open the casket lid and sat up. Camille and Spike had already emerged from their boxes, and stood together in the middle of the car, watching the door, their caskets closed behind them.

Frank stood and shut his, too. Eventually, someone would come to unload them, and having the lids closed might delay the inevitable questions and buy his posse an hour or more to get clear of the station.

The three of them were just starting for the door when it slid open and Stan peered in, his eyes glowing a pale, wintery blue as he searched the interior of the car, using his unusual gift to see in the dim light. He looked as he had the last time they'd met, a skinny young man with a serious expression and hair the color of good, rich soil. Only this time, instead of a coach driver's simple fare, he wore a long, wool coat and thick gloves.

His gaze landed on Frank just as Curtis vaulted past him, into the car. The boy had grown a good bit in the months since Frank's posse had gone back to Hell, adding at least an inch to his height, and filling out a bit through the shoulders and chest, and his thick winter clothes made him look even bigger. He dashed across the floor and flung his arms around Frank's waist, burying his face in the duster for a moment before pushing back and wrinkling his freckled nose.

"Ugh, you guys need some more sleep. You smell like a graveyard."

Frank laughed and looked the boy over from hat to boots.

"You look like Stan's been taking right good care of you, Curtis."

Curtish shrugged. "He's all right, as uncles go."

Camille raised an eyebrow at Stan. "Uncle now, eh? Didn't see that coming."

"I needed a reason to take care of him," the driver answered. "For schools and so on. They need some sort of next-of-kin on their paperwork. Uncle was easiest, since I'm not old enough to be his daddy."

Stan climbed into the freight car, closing the door most of the way behind him.

"Welcome to Albany. I have my stage coach hitched and ready to take you to Dover. Is Batcho here?"

Frank pointed to the back, where the coyote still cowered, growling in the rear corner of his cage. Stan went to him and knelt. Batcho ceased his growling and sniffed cautiously at the hand Stan extended. His ears perked up and he took a half-step forward.

Curtis joined him, and unlike Stan, thrust his hand into the cage, scratching the coyote's ears like he'd done so often the first time they were together.

Batcho relaxed, then, his tongue lolling out and his tail giving a tentative wag.

"Looks like Buzzy was right," Stan said. "The modifications will take some time to settle in. If I understand the old man's instructions right, Batcho should be pretty afraid of you until he figures out you're not really threats."

He examined the padlock and produced a skeleton key from his pocket.

As soon as Stan reached for the padlock again, Batcho backed into the farthest corner of the cage, baring his teeth at Frank and the others. As Stan eased the door open, a low growl crept from the shadows, but Batcho remained frozen, hackles up.

"Easy, old friend." Stan kept his voice low and soothing, and locked his eyes on the coyote's forepaws to avoid eye contact. "These are friends. They won't hurt you."

Batcho sniffed the air and his growl changed to a weak whine. His ears perked forward, but his tail stayed between his legs.

Stan held his fingers just inches from the gleaming teeth, and Batcho sniffed his hand. He relaxed enough to take a hesitant step forward.

It took the better part of fifteen minutes for Stan to coax their guide all the way out, but when Batcho finally emerged, he went to Curtis, behind the three dead people, and stood protectively in front of the boy.

Curtis shrugged. "We got to know each other."

"Batcho has learned to trust Curtis." Stan stood. "Maybe if he sees that Curtis trusts all of you, he'll come to realize you're not threats."

Frank doubted it would be that simple. The coyote's instincts told him Frank, Camille, and Spike were there to kill him. He wouldn't be fooled into trusting them so simply.

Curtis scratched the big coyote's ears, then stepped slowly to Frank. With a soothing word to Batcho, he wrapped his arms around Frank's waist.

Batcho tensed, but didn't move, so Frank eased one arm around Curtis' shoulders.

Batcho reacted so quickly, Frank couldn't have stopped him if his gun hand had been free. Teeth sank into the back of Frank's hand where it rested on Curtis' shoulder. It didn't hurt, but the coyote came away with a strip of skin in his teeth, yellow eyes locked onto Frank and a low growl of warning bubbling in his chest.

Curtis shoved away from Frank and spun to face Batcho, pointing. "Bad! Batcho, no!"

Confusion flicked in Batcho's golden eyes for a moment before he lowered his head and nuzzled it up under the boy's hand.

"No, that won't work." Curtis pulled his hand away, making Batcho's tail return to its hiding place between his legs. "Frank is a friend. No biting!"

The boy spun and stomped from the car, Batcho trailing. As the coyote slipped out the door, he turned one last, baleful glare on Frank, then jumped down.

"That went well," the coachman rubbed his hands together. "What do you say we get moving?"

Frank nodded, still somewhat shaken by Batcho's transformation. "Where are we going?"

Stan led them out into the bright sunlight, all four of them shielding their eyes with their hands. Frank offered Camille a hand down from the car, but the blonde jumped down on her own, giving him a satisfied smile as he watched.

The air outside was even more frigid than it had been in the car, and gave the bright morning sun a pale, bleached look. Despite the total lack of clouds in the sky, the sun offered no warmth. Around them, men and women dressed in suits and dresses shuffled past, most steering a wide path around Frank and his friends. They wore the more formal styles of the east coast, so Frank knew he and his more western-attired friends stood out. And they probably stank, too.

They jogged across the curving tracks of Albany's Union Station, then marched up the granite stairs and through the mammoth stone terminal building with its arches and decorative stone work. Wagons waited for passengers against the curb, while others clattered by on the street, their horses' breath steaming the frigid air as they trotted past.

"Why Albany?" Frank asked. "Wouldn't it have been faster for us to take the train to Boston?"

Stan stood on the curb, looking left and right. Then, he put his fingers in his mouth and whistled, a shrill, almost frightening note that drew down-the-nose looks from several nearby ladies.

"We think Booth is expecting you," Stan answered, still searching the street. "This was safer, and will be almost as quick."

"How would they know we were coming?"

To their right, horses whinnied and a man shouted.

"You gained quite a reputation after how you handled Jesse James," Stan said. "Word apparently got around Hell — and similar circles here — that Hell's Marshal isn't one to be ignored. Booth probably just assumed they'd send you again."

Before Frank could ask more, a team of four horses thundered around a corner, barreling into the street in front of the station, a shining ebony coach behind them. They clattered to a stop in front of Stan and stood, tossing their heads so their mangy manes flapped and swung. They looked better than the last time Frank had seen them. Their fur was mostly intact, and as far as he could tell, none of their flesh had rotted off. But as he looked closer, he saw the faintest hint of flame in their eyes, and recognized the pure hatred behind them.

"Same team as before?" Frank asked.

Stan nodded.

"Then, we might beat the trains."

"We think we know where Booth's former betrothed is. We should get to Dover by sundown, so we can look for her when we get there."

"Any sign of our prey for this little trip?"

Stan shook his head. "We've seen nothing of John Wilkes Booth's spirit, but if he's half the actor they say he is, he might be able to pass for a living person pretty well. Still, Curtis here has been on the lookout with that gift of his."

Frank nodded. Curtis' ability to see people who

were possessed could help them. Stan watched as the others clambered aboard the stage.

They passed a group of workers taking down garland from the lamp posts outside, and Frank found his smooth-soled boots slipped a bit on the icy sidewalk

"Stan, what's the date today?"

"January 16th, Marshal. 1893."

Frank shook his head. He'd been in Hell only six months since snagging Jesse James. It had felt like eternity.

* * *

The coach and horses carried them steadily northeast, bounding effortlessly down highways and back country roads. Even cloaked in the whites and grays of winter, the northeast held more color than the American southwest, where Frank had spent most of his adult years.

As the deep greens of pine and spruce sped past, mingled with winter's pallor, Frank tried not to think about the underworld test that had placed him in a similarly cold and frozen place, when he'd faced off against the monster his wife had become.

He shivered, and Camille slid closer to him.

"Since you can't seem to keep yourself warm, I suppose I can lend you some body heat."

The horses, being steeds from Hell, didn't need to stop or rest or even eat. So, while they didn't run at their full speed to avoid attracting attention, they did run nonstop, not even working up a lather by the time they slowed to a trot on the outskirts of Dover, New Hampshire.

The sun had started its nightly fall, lengthening shadows across Silver Street as the group moved east.

The streets teemed with people, despite the bitter cold. These were hearty folks, dressed in heavy wool coats, with fur-lined hats and mittens to keep them warm. But they walked with urgency, doing their evening chores quickly to slip back home.

Stan guided the stage down the street at a cautious pace now, letting pedestrians dodge out of the way or meander to the side. A few minutes later, he swung right on Central Avenue and stopped outside a three-story brick building with chimneys on either end and shutters on each window.

The driver hopped down and jogged to Frank's door.

"Here we are, 189 Central Avenue. This is the Hale residence, where Lucy Hale—now Lucy Chandler, having married a Senator named Chandler—is supposedly staying while her husband is in Washington."

Frank dismounted the coach, with Camille on his left and Spike on his right. The three of them took one step toward the Chandler residence before Stan moved in front of them, blocking the walkway.

He cleared his throat. "Uhm, this might be a good time for me and the boy to do the talking. You three…well, you're still a might…"

"Dead," Camille finished for him. "We're likely to frighten these nice, polite New Hampshire folk."

Stan gave them an apologetic look, but nodded.

Frank grunted and looked at his friends. While they'd healed on the train, blue lines still ran from Camille's lips, her eyes glassy and bloodshot. And Spike's nose had a rotten spot on its tip.

"I reckon maybe you're right. We'll wait here for now, but any sign of Booth and we're comin' in, guns blazing."

Stan sighed as he and Curtis strode up the icy stone walk toward the door.

They knocked and a maid opened the door. She and Stan spoke in hushed tones for a moment, too low for Frank to hear. A guttural growl made him look over his shoulder to find Batcho sitting on the driver's seat, golden eyes riveted on Frank and his friends. He glanced from them to Stan and back again, as if looking for permission to attack.

A minute later, the maid closed the door and Stan brought Curtis back to the stage.

"She said that Lucy left this afternoon," he explained, blowing into his hands and rubbing them together. "Said she got a letter from someone, got real upset, and took her personal carriage into town. Muttered something about meeting an old friend."

"Did she tell you what was in the letter?" Frank asked.

Stan shook his head. "Lucy burned it as soon as she read it, and while the maid apparently tried to read the ashes after Lucy had gone, there wasn't enough left."

"She's going to meet Booth," Frank said, rubbing his temples with ice-cold knuckles. "And now we have no idea where she is."

"Dover's not that big a town," Stan replied. "We ought to be able to track her down by her carriage."

"Curtis, could you tell if the maid was...like us?"

Curtis nodded. "She's normal."

"Can we have Batcho sniff around for anyone who isn't fully alive anymore?"

Stan gave the coyote on his bench seat a dubious look. "We could, but I'm not sure it would do any good. Look at him. He's completely focused on you three right now. I'm pretty sure a demon could walk up, tweak his nose, and he still wouldn't notice."

Sure enough, Batcho's fierce, gold gaze hadn't wandered from Frank and his group. It unnerved Frank more than a little.

Frank looked away, careful not to make eye contact with the beast. He knew enough about coyotes to know a challenge would be met with ferocity, and he needed Batcho on their side as soon as possible.

He shrugged. "All right, then. Let's get to searching."

CHAPTER THREE

They started asking around at the train station, but no one had seen Lucy Chandler, so they took their search to the streets of Dover. Stan and Spike went north on foot, with Batcho trailing them in the shadows, while Frank, Camille, and Curtis walked south along Central Avenue, posing as a family. Frank was thankful for the frigid weather, as it allowed him and Camille to cover their faces under the guise of staying warm, hiding their deathly appearance from passersby.

They were passing a Western Union office when Frank had an idea. Waving the other two to follow, he stepped inside. A balding man in suspenders and spectacles looked up from behind a counter and studied them with a guarded look. Camille started to remove her scarf, but Frank put his hand on her forearm.

The little man squinted at them, but forced a smile. "What can I do for you?"

"We were supposed to meet a friend of ours here." Frank spoke through his kerchief. "Lucy Chandler?"

The little man's eyes skipped over each of them, and he adjusted his glasses with slender fingers. For a moment, he scrunched his brow down, as if considering. Frank slid back the flap of his duster, exposing his pistol. The man sighed.

"She left about a half-hour ago," he told them. "Sent her husband a telegram and went on her way with some handsome fellow."

Camille and Frank exchanged a glance.

"What fellow?" Camille asked.

Clearly suspicious now, the wispy man crossed his arms over his chest and gave the group a hard stare.

"What did this gentleman look like?" Frank asked. "Mrs. Chandler could be in danger."

The clerk cleared his throat and adjusted his bowtie.

"Like I said, handsome fellow. Dark, curly hair. Moustache. I've seen him at the theater before. I think he's an actor."

"Do you know what she told her husband?"

"That information is confidential. What did you say your names were, again?"

Frank's hand drifted toward the six-shooter on his hip, but Camille's hand on his elbow stopped him.

"This ain't Tombstone," she whispered.

Frank grumbled.

The clerk peered around Frank and pointed outside. "That's him, right there. The actor."

Frank wheeled in time to see a handsome man in a black suit turn and stride away. His dark, curly hair was carefully sculpted, and as he looked back over his shoulder, he twirled the end of a finely groomed moustache.

Then, he disappeared into the crowd.

Frank and his friends dashed out the door, but none could find the man. They searched for several minutes, then Frank pulled them into a side alley and drummed his fingers on his chin.

"Curtis, did you get a long enough look to know if he was possessed?"

Curtis nodded. "He is."

"Well," Frank mused. "I'd say old Booth has taken up residence in someone similar to himself."

"Makes sense," Curtis said. "Being a handsome actor worked before. He's hoping the same soup recipe that warmed her heart before will do so again."

Camille gave the boy a flat stare. "Soup recipe?"

Curtis shrugged. "Stan thinks I should talk better."

The hooker rolled her eyes.

"All right then," Frank told them. "We know what our man looks like. And he's got Lucy. Let's find the others and let them know."

They found Stan and Spike a few minutes later and filled them in. When Frank finished, Stan scratched the stubble on his chin.

"Doesn't make sense, Marshal. For three days, Curtis and I have been watching Lucy's house, but coming up drier than a watering hole in the Mojave. Why the sudden appearance when all of you get to town?"

"Might just be coincidence," Spike suggested.

"When it comes to Hell," Stan told him, "I don't believe in coincidence."

They split up again, with Frank and Curtis pairing up, while Spike and Stan stuck together. Against Frank's better judgment, Camille went off alone.

She batted her eyelashes. "If one of you is along, flirting for information is impossible."

Frank chose not to tell her that with her smell and the blue lines around her mouth, she'd be more likely to scare a man than attract him. He knew how fast she was with the Bowie knife.

"Just be careful," he told her. "And if you see Booth, come get us. Don't try handling him on your own."

She nodded and swayed off south on Central Avenue.

The sun had dipped below Dover's low roofs and tree line, and electric lamps flickered and buzzed to life, lighting the street with an orange glow.

Frank walked with Stan east on Sixth Street, wincing at the rigidity in his legs. Moving them felt like dragging sandbags.

"We need to get somewhere and warm up soon," he told Stan. "Need this old corpse to thaw."

Stan was about to answer when a woman slipped from the shadows and glided toward them. She wore the multi-colored patchwork dress of a gypsy, with a thick, wool cloak over in the deepest midnight blue. Rings glittered on every finger, and heavy earrings tugged at each earlobe.

"Tell your fortune?" Her voice slid to them, throaty and accented.

Frank held up a hand. "My fortune's already been met."

She stepped back, eyes going wide and her mouth forming a silent "O" under her hooked beak of a nose. Frank checked the kerchief around his face, finding it firmly in place, yet still, the woman looked at him like he was a ghost.

"I know the one you seek," she whispered.

Frank stopped dead in his tracks.

"What do you mean?"

She leaned in close, voice slipping through her gold-capped teeth like silk.

"I told his fortune last night, on this very street. The one they sent you to kill."

Frank tensed, and felt Stan's hand on his shoulder.

"She's a con artist," he mumbled.

It was probably true, but something about the deep dusk of the woman's eyes roped him and pulled him in.

"If that's true, tell me where he went so I can send him back where he belongs."

She shook her head slowly, one corner of her mouth turning upward.

"His fortune will mean nothing to you. You should be asking for your own."

Frank narrowed his eyes, peering into the chasms of hers, then nodded.

"I'm listening."

She stuck out her hand, and Stan rolled his eyes.

"Told you. She's just after your money."

But Frank ignored him, digging a dime from his pocket and placing it in the woman's bejeweled hand.

She took his hand and spread his fingers wide, tracing the lines on his palm with a sharp fingernail. For a moment, she looked perplexed, then she dropped his hand and stepped back, eyes wide as crystal balls.

For a moment, he thought she might run, her lips quivering. Then, she recovered and stepped close again.

"Darkness swirls around you, and shadows want you destroyed. You will swim in a lake of blood, but if you don't, others will spill an ocean of it. You are all that stands between order and chaos, and chains pull you toward both. Those who need you most also want you gone.

"Be cautious, Marshal Butcher. Things are not as they seem, and your true enemy is still hidden." Her eyes darted about and her lip trembled. "I've said too much already. You've gotten more than you paid for."

She wheeled and strode away, disappearing into the alley from which she'd come.

"Well, that was enlightening," Stan said. "And a total waste of ten cents. Are you ready to start looking now?"

Frank grunted, but stared after the woman. Her fortune had been dangerously close to his dream. His stomach knotted as he thought about the killing he'd have to do.

"How'd she know my name?" he asked.

Stan shrugged and moved off down the street.

An hour later, Frank's hand twitched near the handle to his pistol and his boots drummed a rhythm on the wooden floor of the small tavern off Central Avenue. Before him sat a half-empty whiskey glass, its top half dumped in a potted plant beside the table, the remainder taunting Frank, almost begging him to drink it.

Beside him, Stan took a sip from a mug of beer and leaned back until the cheap wooden chair creaked.

The tavern was mostly empty, understandable since it was a Monday night, and the few patrons present had settled into easy conversation. In a back corner, two old men played chess, their drinks untouched on the table by the board, and at the bar, a younger man in a gray suit flirted with a slender redhead still wearing her white wool jacket.

And through it all danced the sound of a fiddle, played by a boy about Curtis' age, sitting on a bar stool near the front window, trying to attract patrons.

Frank reached for his glass, but stopped when he

felt Stan's eyes on him. Then, he slid the tumbler away and groaned.

"It's bad enough we gotta run around playing detective, asking questions and watching people, but I can't even have a drink to make it more interesting."

Stan put his foot up on one of the four empty chairs around their table.

"Don't let me stop you from imbibing. I'm interested in seeing just what it does to someone in your...condition."

One corner of his mouth turned up.

"Enjoy it while you can, son," Frank mumbled. "It's bound to go south before too long. We all die, but only some of us get to come back."

The door opened, jingling a small bell, and Camille stepped in with a rush of frigid air. She still wore the gray trousers and the loose, buttoned shirt, but hadn't removed the makeup from her face, leaving her lips bright red and her cheeks blushed. The dark circles under her eyes now looked like eye shadow, and her golden curls tumbled out from under the floppy brown hat she'd plopped on her head.

She caught Frank looking and for just an instant, her expression softened. She looked like she was on the verge of a smile, as if one might spontaneously break across her painted lips. Then, her eyes went cold and she frowned as she crossed the room to him.

"What are you looking at, gunfighter?"

"You look right pretty, Camille." He couldn't meet the frigid ice of her gaze.

"Well, don't get used to it," she responded. "I just thought it might make me look more normal for now. Until my body catches up."

"Where's Batcho?" Stan waved the bartender over.

"Chasing a cat the last I saw." Curtis yawned.

The three of them took the empty chairs, Camille ordering a sarsaparilla for Curtis, with shots of whiskey for her and Spike. The bartender studied her a moment, eyebrows raised, then twisted one end of his handlebar moustache and walked off to get their order.

"We found some information." Curtis barely contained his excitement. Feeling needed was important to a boy whose family had sold him to a mining company. "You told us to look for anyone acting out of the ordinary, and it seems an entire family kind of went off the tracks last night. Wandered into a tattoo parlor like they were drunk, only none of 'em smelled like liquor."

He paused as the bartender delivered their drinks. As soon as the man wandered off, Spike picked up the tale.

"The Hammond family—Marybeth, John, Joseph, William, and Stephen—all showed up at a tattoo place on Baker Street, wanting their initials tattooed on their hands."

"What's so odd about that?" Frank asked.

"First of all," Camille said, "they weren't their initials. They were someone else's. Most importantly, John Hammond had the initials 'JWB' inked on the back of his hand."

"John Wilkes Booth," Stan muttered. "Seems like a stupid thing to do when you know we're chasing you."

"I agree." Frank was tempted again to take a drink, but kept himself from reaching for the glass with a surge of willpower. "Mr. Booth must be very confident in his ability to beat us, or he's taunting us."

"There's more," Curtis added. "John Hammond is an actor. A particularly handsome one, at that. And now the whole family's disappeared."

Stan whistled. "Well, that sure sounds like our man."

Something caught Frank's attention. At the front of the tavern, looking in the plate glass window, was a man dressed in a dull, gray suit. A bowler sat on his head, and his round face was little more than a nebulous shape, with no features visible through the frosted pane. Still, even without seeing his eyes, Frank knew for sure the man was staring right at him. Through him, even.

Then he blinked, and the man was gone.

"Frank?" Camille reached out and touched his hand, her eyes following his gaze to the front window.

"I need sleep."

"We all do," Spike said. "Let's find someplace to hole up and rebuild a bit."

"I'll find us a room," Curtis volunteered, jumping to his feet.

"Not so fast, boy." Frank held up his hand. "This isn't the west. A hotel here'll cost a pretty penny, I'd wager."

Stan nodded.

Camille checked the purse at her waist and Spike fished through his pockets. Both came up empty. Frank managed to pull a pair of quarters from his duster pocket, but every other pocket was empty. He offered the coins to Stan, feeling sheepish.

"Looks like the judges didn't think of everything," he muttered.

Stan rolled his eyes. "And those of us in the 'Arcane Assistant' field don't make enough to cover nice hotel rooms. You'll have to make do with whatever I can afford."

"I don't suppose you can pick a pocket?" Frank looked at Curtis while he spoke.

The boy shook his head. "Weren't any pockets worth

pickin' in the mines. Miners get paid less than Arcane Assistants."

Frank nodded and patted Stan on the shoulder. "Do what you can."

As they rose, Frank's gaze was drawn again to the window at the front of the tavern, where he swore the shape of a man in gray stood for a moment before fading. Camille caught him looking again and waved her hand in front of his eyes.

Frank tore his eyes from the window. "Let's go."

The second-story room was barely big enough for the double bed, small table, and tattered, cushioned chair that faced a cracked window that overlooked the street below. Lacking electricity, their light came from two old-fashioned oil lamps, one on the table and the other on a night stand by the bed. The still-frigid air inside smelled of tobacco and tasted like dust.

Frank kneeled by an iron wood stove and was grateful to see the proprietor had at least set it up with kindling and wood, even if they hadn't lit it. He struck a match and tossed it in, watching the wadded-up newspaper catch and smelling its acrid smoke.

Camille stood over the bed, nose wrinkled, as she stared down at the fraying blanket and yellowing sheets.

"Probably has fleas or lice," she murmured.

"Probably both," Frank added. "But I don't think either will bother dead people."

She cocked her head to one side, then shrugged and lay on top of the sheets, pulling up a ratty, wool blanket over herself. Spike winced and folded himself into a stiff sitting position against the wall by the stove, a bit closer than Frank thought wise.

"You know dead flesh'll burn faster than live stuff, right?"

"At this point, at least I wouldn't be cold anymore."

Frank tossed a log onto the now-crackling fire and stood. He glanced at the bed where Camille lay. As if sensing his eyes on her, Camille's hand drifted under the blanket to rest on the Bowie knife on her hip.

Frank sighed and settled into the chair, turning it so the window was on his right and the heat from the stove blasted him in the face.

It seemed he'd no sooner drifted off to sleep than the door burst open. Frank jumped to his feet, drawing a good bit slower than usual. Spike shot to his knees, leveling the Winchester at the door. But Camille moved faster than either of them, flying from the bed like a banshee, pressing her Bowie's gleaming green blade against Stan's throat. Frank and Spike lowered their guns, but Camille didn't let up, her blade digging into the soft flesh over Stan's left jugular.

Camille's eyes held the look of a cornered colt, wild and dangerous, frightened beyond reason. Stan remained calm, hands held out before him, but his blue eyes glowed their unnatural light and the fingers on his left hand danced in a series of gestures that Frank knew weren't random.

"Camille, it's Stan," Frank told her, putting himself in her peripheral vision but being careful not to get too close. If he crowded her, things would end badly for Stan. "He's a friend."

Her lips curled back, baring her teeth as her voice came in a snarl.

"Thought you'd sneak in on me, huh? Thought maybe you'd catch me sleeping, maybe in my nightclothes?"

She pressed the knife harder on Stan's throat. Frank tensed…if she drew blood, Stan was done.

"Camille, please." Stan's voice was calm as a summer pond. His fingers still danced. "I don't want to hurt you. We're friends."

His eyes flashed brighter, and a glow started to surround his hand. Frank hadn't seen much of what Stan could do with his powers, but he suspected he was very capable.

"I ain't friends with any *man!*" Pure hatred dripped from her words like blood from fangs, and a trickle of green light ran from the blade's edge down Stan's neck. If she managed to get it into his blood, she'd wipe his soul from existence.

Frank took a step closer and she glared at him, snarling again. "I'll kill him! No one's touching me tonight!"

Frank opened his mouth to speak, but Curtis slipped into the room behind Stan, staring up at the hooker with his big, brown eyes. Confusion danced across Camille's expression as she looked down at him.

"Camille, don't hurt him," Curtis said. He reached out with a slow, deliberate motion and let his fingers rest light as snowflakes on her elbow. "He's my friend."

Camille's face scrunched together, as if she were in pain. Lowering the knife from Stan's throat, she shook her head and dropped to the edge of the bed. Curtis scooted to sit next to her and Stan straightened, dropping his hand to his side. His fingers stopped moving and the blue light disappeared from his hand and eyes.

Frank nodded at his hand.

Stan shrugged. "She needed more sleep. I was going to give it to her."

Frank nodded and closed the door. Camille had put her head in her hands, golden curls falling like curtains around her face.

"I was dreaming. Something awful, from my life. I thought—"

She gave Stan a helpless look.

"It's okay." Stan waved it off. "Happens."

She nodded and put her face back in her hands.

Silence wrapped the group for a moment, and they all looked at the floor. Then Curtis popped up from the bed, brimming with excitement, breaking the tense silence.

"We found Lucy!"

Frank and Stan exchanged a glance, and the driver nodded. "Well, we found out where she's going."

"It's my story!" Curtis planted his hands on his hips. "I found out, so I get to tell it!"

Even Camille chuckled at the boy's sudden humor, and the bleak mood in the room lifted.

Frank put a hand on Curtis' shoulder. "Well, tell us, then."

"She's with the Hammond family. They took her to the train station and they hopped a car out of town."

"Where were they going?" Frank asked.

"Newport, Rhode Island. It seems Mr. Booth is taking his lover to a vacation at the Aquidneck Hotel for a night of wooing."

Frank grabbed his duster off the chair, and the others bustled to grab their things.

"Looks like we're going to Rhode Island," Frank said. "Good detective work, boys."

CHAPTER FOUR

Even from his spot on the driver's bench, Frank knew they were being followed as they clip-clopped down a dirt road north of Boston. They'd traveled all night, Hell's steeds needing neither rest nor food, and had approached the city as the sun spilled its glory over the eastern horizon. Now, as they kept a brisk pace south, the horses' breath steaming in the crackling-cold air, Frank could sense the man in gray behind them.

Frank had tried alerting Stan to the man's presence twice during the night, but both times, the gray man disappeared before Stan could get a glimpse with his glowing blue eyes. Two things about the gray man bothered Frank more than anything else. First, he'd kept up with them through the night. No one kept pace with Stan's carriage or the beasts that drew it. Second, and even more alarming, the stranger had done so seemingly on foot.

The last time, Frank had spotted the man standing a hundred yards or so behind them, hair billowing in the frigid breeze, hands in his long, gray overcoat. His eyes seemed to absorb the darkness around them, and his skin shone like pearl in the moonlight.

Still, the man had disappeared before Stan could turn around. The driver had frowned at Frank's description of what he saw, worrying the gunfighter even more.

Even Batcho, who trotted along in the tree line, looked back from time to time and snarled.

"How fast can this rig go?" Frank asked, as the morning sun warmed his shoulders and back.

Stan shrugged. "You were in it that night in Missouri. Fast. Damned fast."

"See that bend up there?" Frank pointed to a curve a hundred yards or so ahead of them, where the road disappeared to their right, passing behind the tall pines and oaks that lined it, gray as smoke.

Stan nodded.

"Get around it as fast as possible and keep going," Frank ordered. "Don't stop for nothing."

Stan raised his eyebrows, but snapped the reins.

"Ha! Git up!"

The coach leapt forward, nearly tossing Frank from the bench. He held on to a rail at the edge of the seat, his other hand keeping his hat on his head as the wind tried to tear it away. They went so fast, Frank's face stiffened up, his lips refusing to work when he told them to, his eyes watering until ice crystals twinkled in his vision.

Spike stuck his head out a window from the cabin. "What's going on, Marshal?"

"Just stay inside. I need a rabbit, and you're all it."

"Being followed?"

"Looks like."

Spike pulled his head back inside just as they rounded the bend, the coach leaning dangerously to the left. Frank looked down, measuring the distance and their speed. The right side wheels lifted off the ground, threatening to topple the coach on its side.

As soon as they were around the bend, he stood.

"Go a minute or so down the road," he told Stan, "then come on back and see if I've gone back to Hell."

And with that, Frank flung himself off the carriage.

He hit feet-first, pain rifling up his left leg all the way to his hip, and he tucked into a roll, absorbing the rest of the shock as he tumbled off the road and into the tall weeds along its edge. He belly-crawled back among the trees, ignoring the fire in his leg, and rose to his knees. He thought about drawing his pistol, but something made him pull out the lariat Buzzy had given him. He'd need to ask this fella some questions before sending him back to the Boss-man.

Batcho slinked into the trees beside him, yellow eyes baleful as he crouched and let out a low growl, green drool dripping. Then, the man in gray appeared in the street.

He wasn't much to look at, with his low forehead and deep-set eyes, but he carried himself with purpose, and with confidence.

That's when Frank noticed his boots. Polished black leather with brass buckles, they stood out from the rest of his drab form, something darker than gray.

More importantly, they didn't touch the ground. He hovered an inch or two over the road, perfectly still, feet planted in mid-air.

Frank stifled a gasp as the gray man stepped off toward them, feet still not touching the dirt. As he passed their position, Frank again shrugged off the agony in his leg and braced himself for a bullrush. Batcho, however, was faster. The coyote sprang from cover and crouched in front of their follower, teeth bared, hackles up.

The gray man froze, his hands coming up before him. A soft white glow blossomed around his fingers, as if the winter sun had been captured and held as a weapon.

"Foul creature of Satan!" The gray man's voice was high-pitched, almost nasally, and tinged with a soft, southern lilt. "Go on, git outta here before I have to smite you."

Batcho held his head low, fur forming a sharp ridge along his neck and shoulders, a dollop of green drool hanging from his lip. The gray man didn't take his eyes off the coyote, so Frank moved to the side of the road, just a couple of yards behind the man's right shoulder. He held the lasso at his waist, ready to throw.

As if sensing him, the gray man started to turn his head, but Batcho growled and edged forward, forcing him to keep his attention on the coyote.

Frank heaved the looped end of the lasso, and his motion alerted the man. He dodged to the left, the lasso falling limp in the dirt. Before the gray man could face Frank, though, Batcho launched himself at him, crashing into his chest with a flash of claws and teeth. The coyote drove the gray man to the ground, and when his back hit, it most definitely struck the frozen dirt.

"Get off me!"

He thrust his hands forward, and pale light flashed. Batcho sailed through the air, disappearing into the trees with a crash and a yelp, but he'd bought Frank time. This time, the lasso fell around the gray man's outstretched hands, and Frank pulled it tight. The man's eyes popped wide and his mouth opened as if he might scream, but instead, he scrunched his features as if biting back agony, took a deep breath, and rose to his feet.

"You do not want to do this," he warned, voice dropping lower. "It's the biggest mistake you'll ever make."

"Why's that?"

Frank gave to rope a terse tug and grinned as the man staggered forward, his feet dragging on the rock-hard dirt.

"You don't want to anger my boss."

"Reckon I'll worry about that later. What's your name and why are you following us?"

As he spoke, the sound of Stan's carriage clattered back toward them. Batcho stumbled from the trees, shaking his head, and the gray man grinned. He looked at Frank, his eyes going from brown to ebony in a heartbeat.

"My name is Sergeant Boston Corbett, and you'd better start worrying about my boss now. See, Marshal Butcher, you didn't capture just anyone. You roped yourself an angel. Which means my boss—"

"Is still not my problem."

He gave the rope another tug to remind Corbett who was in charge. At the moment, anyway.

* * *

They trotted into Newport around dinner time that evening, the air so bitter cold, it felt like a whip on Frank's exposed skin. The setting sun was little more than a pale orange disk hanging over the frozen surface of Narragansett Bay. Even the sharp tang of salt water smelled cold here.

As they moved south along Bellevue, Frank felt out of place. As in Dover, these were different-looking houses than he was used to from the west. Instead of clapboard and dark woods, these homes were painted, usually white, with shutters and porches, white picket fences separating neighbor from neighbor. Most of those people stayed inside, sitting around well-lit dining tables, but a few passed on the street, dressed in long coats designed more for style than warmth. None looked up from the cobblestones long enough to notice anything odd about the coach that passed them. Either that, or they ignored the fact that a western-style stage coach, done all in lacquer and driven by men with guns, had invaded their frozen paradise.

Still, Frank had drawn the curtains on Stan's stage so no one could see Boston Corbett lashed to one seat. Spike and Camille sat across from him, her fingering her Bowie while the bartender kept his Winchester at the ready.

Something about Corbett didn't add up, as if he were telling the truth, but not the whole of it, lying by omission. For his part, Corbett hadn't spoken again since issuing his initial warning. Instead, he sat rigid as a rifle, wincing as if the lasso from Hell hurt. Sweat beaded on his brow, and his pallid skin grew pink and feverish.

Frank didn't rightly care if the man was an angel. Frank and his people answered to the Boss-man downstairs, not the one in Heaven. He didn't know much about how Heaven worked, but he didn't imagine its Boss-man cared whether he took Booth back to Hell. And that's what Frank intended to do.

"We'll make a line for the Aquidneck House Hotel," Stan said from beside him on the bench. "The sooner we get there, the sooner we can evaluate things."

"And get to shootin'," Curtis added, grinning up at Frank from the other side. "To the part Frank's good at."

Frank frowned and turned his attention to Curtis.

"You're shivering, son. Why don't you ride in the cabin, out of the wind?"

"I'd rather be up here, with you."

An unfamiliar pang filled Frank's chest, a tightening like a hangman's noose around his heart. And he remembered the last time he'd felt it.

"You'd best get below, anyway," he told the boy. "You'll get sick up here, and if you're sick, you're no good to the team."

Curtis sighed and started to climb to the cabin when Stan reined in hard, sliding the wagon to a stop. It took Frank a moment to see why, but when he did, he reached for his pistol.

They had stopped beside a park, an open space of grass and trees at the corner of Bellevue and Mills Road. Benches stood like iron sentries around the grounds, but it was a structure at the center of the park that drew their attention.

Standing like an ancient fortress, a stone-and-mortar tower crouched, its roof long gone, its arched entrances open. Surrounded by a low fence, the tower looked older that the rest of the town, older than most things Frank had seen in America. It stood out, like Frank and his posse, as something rougher and less cultured.

Inside, visible through the arches, stood another man in gray. He was surrounded by a swirling cloud of mist, masking his features, but Frank caught sight of a handlebar moustache, and eyes as cold as the air around them.

"Now you're in trouble," Corbett announced from

inside the coach. "That there's my partner, and he don't look real happy."

He was right. The second gray man hefted a rifle up to his shoulder and took aim at Frank. Pale, golden light oozed from the rifle's breech.

"You'll want to release my man, now." The voice thundered through the park. "This rifle is loaded with rounds designed for folks like you."

Frank hopped down, keeping his hand near his pistol. He'd heard that voice before, but couldn't place it.

"What do you mean, 'like us?'"

"You know darn well what I mean. You're Hell's Marshal, and that there's your posse."

Spike and Camille climbed out, the hooker shoving Corbett before her. He winced as the lasso bit into his skin. As soon as he stabilized himself, Camille grabbed him from behind and pressed the blade of her Bowie against his throat, a rivulet of deathly green running down his skin.

The figure took aim at Camille, and something told Frank that if he pulled the trigger, she'd be back in Hell before he could even draw.

"Your partner here was following us." He kept his eyes locked on the second gray man. "Maybe, if you explain why, we'll let him go and we can all be on our way."

The mist continued to swirl around the man's rigid form, hiding his face as the familiar voice rang out.

"We seek the same people you do. We want to stop Booth and his people from doing whatever damage they're after here in the living world. We simply represent different bosses, you and us."

Frank squinted, trying to penetrate the mist. Stan moved up beside him, his own Sharps rifle at the ready.

"Do I know him?" the driver whispered.

Frank faced the gray man. "This one claims he's an angel. That make you one, too?"

Something changed in the gray man's posture then, a slight unwinding of tension, and his attention shifted ever so slightly to Boston Corbett.

"He misspoke." Disappointment and more than a little irritation leaked through his words. "We are not angels. Yet."

"Then, what in the Sam Hell are you? And who?"

The gray man lowered his rifle and motioned them forward.

"I won't harm you."

"Cover us," Frank told Stan. "If he lifts that Sharps again..."

"I know what to do. Just not sure my gun will make a difference with this one."

Spike raised his Winchester to his shoulder, keeping the muzzle down.

"Mine will."

Frank nodded to Camille, and the two of them edged forward, keeping Corbett between them and the gray man. Corbett's demeanor had changed from one of almost arrogant confidence to uncertainty and hesitation. His eyes darted from the other gray man to Frank and back again, and despite the frigid air that stiffened Frank's limbs, Corbett sweated like a hard-run race horse.

As they neared, the mist around the second gray man started to fade, thinning and dissipating into the air. As soon as it revealed his face, Frank sucked in a breath.

A long, smoke-colored overcoat hung from his shoulders, and a bowler the color of granite topped his head. His moustache had been finely oiled, and twisted into spirals at the ends, and his stone-gray eyes studied Frank with a cold detachment.

On his coat hung a shield-shaped detective's badge.

"Mills," Frank whispered.

Curtis burst from the coach and streaked past them, wrapping his arms around the one-time Pinkerton man's waist.

For the first time, the gray man smiled.

Frank motioned to Spike to lower his rifle, but he said nothing to Camille. Just because Mills had helped them during their last job didn't mean he was on their side again this time. If he was an angel, Frank had the feeling they were no longer friends.

As Curtis eased away from Mills, Batcho trotted from a nearby bush and sniffed the detective's hand, tail wagging.

Frank took a cautious step forward. "I wondered where you went. I guess the judges decided differently for you."

Mills studied him.

"Not exactly, Marshal. It's a might hard to explain, but Sergeant Corbett and me, we're...on probation. He misstated our status, as he's known to do. We're being tested. If we complete our assignment, we become full-fledged angels."

"And that assignment is what, exactly?"

Mills glanced around the little park. Several bystanders had stopped to gawk at the men with drawn guns.

"What do you say we retire to our hotel room, where we might talk in some privacy?"

"Sounds like a good idea."

"You can release Mr. Corbett," Mills told Camille. "I promise, he'll do you no harm. He has some atoning to do for being less than truthful, anyway."

Corbett paled visibly and looked at his feet.

Frank nodded to Camille and she released the other gray man, slipping the lasso off his wrists. Corbett hung his head and moved to his partner's side.

"If you'll follow me," Mills said, "I'll show you where we're staying."

CHAPTER FIVE

Frank was jealous. Apparently, Heaven's budget was considerably better than Hell's, based on the room Mills and Corbett had secured.

Located at the end of a street lined with flickering gas lamps, the gray building with neatly arranged shutters and an ample porch almost seemed to open its arms to guests, welcoming the sailors and sea captains who lounged around the first-floor common room. The sweet scent of their pipe smoke wove itself around the tables and chairs, dancing near the few electric light fixtures and hovering near oil lamps. It teased Frank's senses, making him wonder if he could smoke and get away with it. He couldn't drink or eat, but maybe being dead would allow him a puff of tobacco.

But Mills didn't offer the possibility, ushering them

through the packed room toward the stairs. No one seemed to take notice, each sailor seemingly lost in the sea of drink before him.

Mills took them to a room at the end of a long hallway, unlocking the door with a skeleton key, then pausing a moment with his head bowed and his hands flat on the gleaming wood. Frank looked at Stan.

"Warding spell," the driver explained.

"We don't use spells. We're not Warlocks." Corbett spat out the last word like stale bread.

Mills wheeled and shot his partner a withering glare.

"'Judge not lest ye be judged,'" he quoted, making Corbett glance at the floor. "And remember—we *are* being judged here."

He pushed the door open and ushered the group inside. Frank had left Batcho outside to avoid attention, but he still worried their group would be too large for a small hotel room.

He saw now his concern was misplaced. The cavernous room was brighter than any he'd ever seen, with oil lamps, electric bulbs, candles, and even a chandelier hanging from the ceiling emitting more light than they should have. The room was so bright, he shielded his eyes.

"My apologies for the brightness," Mills said. "We tend to like it brighter than most, and our Boss-man sees to it we have a nice, light place to rest our heads at night."

"So this light," Stan stammered, "it's…from him?"

Mills laughed and shook his head. "No, it's not divine, if that's what you mean. We just use his gifts to enhance what light sources we have. It kind of helps us to rebuild our strength, like sleep helps Frank and his friends."

Corbett entered last and clicked the door closed behind him. The room featured a four-poster bed against one wall, with expensive linens and filmy material hanging around it. Floral patterned wallpaper reflected the light, and wainscoting stretched from the hand-carved chair rail to the gleaming hardwood floors.

Frank instinctively moved to a set of French doors at the opposite end of the room and peered out into the growing night. A small balcony stood outside, with white-painted furniture and a striped canopy overhead.

"You needn't worry, Marshal." Mills eased the curtain closed and motioned for Frank to sit in one of four cozy-looking Queen Anne chairs that sat around a small table. "This room is quite secure. No one will see in from outside, nor will they hear our discussions."

"I'm more worried about Booth or his people paying us a visit. They have to know we're coming by now."

Mills nodded and sat across from him. Camille and Spike stood behind Frank, like guardians, while Stan and Curtis remained near the door.

Corbett took a seat beside his partner. Mills sighed.

"The gentleman you've already met is Sergeant Thomas 'Boston ' Corbett. In life, he shot John Wilkes Booth, so he seemed like the perfect choice for this mission. Or so I thought."

Corbett's cockiness withered and his shoulders slouched. He looked again at the tops of his polished boots.

"Come on, Charlie. You're not gonna hold that against me, are you?"

"You lied about us being angels," Mills replied. "And I ain't the one holding anything against you, Boston. The Head Honcho sees everything."

"This is all good and nice," Frank interrupted, "but it doesn't tell me why you two were following our little posse. What stake does Heaven have in Booth being recaptured? Is Lucy that important?"

Mills and Corbett looked at one another, as if a silent telegraph had passed between them. Then, Mills cleared his throat and paced the room.

"They didn't exactly tell us everything. Head Honcho's kind of like that—says it's something about free will or tampering with events or some such. He just told us to eliminate Booth before he causes too much trouble.

"If we do that, we both become full-fledged angels."

"There's gotta be more than that." Stan's eyes narrowed. For a moment, Frank thought he might use his power to try and see Mills in a different way, but his eyes never glowed. "I find it hard to believe Heaven is involved for a couple of rogue spirits trying to re-kindle an old flame."

Mills nodded and put his hands in the pockets of his gray, wool pants, exposing the ivory-white handles of two British revolvers under his coat. Both gave off a yellow glow.

"We suspect he's up to something more nefarious, too, but we can't figure out what."

"How did Heaven's Head Honcho even know these crooks got out? Our Boss-man isn't even aware of it."

"I wouldn't be so sure of that." Mills' forehead furrowed. "I'd bet your Boss-man knows a good bit more than those slippery justices let on. And how else would we find out? We have spies in Hell, of course.

"If he's really up to something big, it might take all of us to stop him."

That made everyone in Frank's group exchange

glances.

Frank studied the one-time detective for a moment, then nodded.

"You helped us with Jesse James' soul, and shot straight then. I don't suppose going to Heaven would make you any less honest of a man, so we welcome your help."

Mills winced, and Corbett chuckled.

"We can't exactly help you," Mills explained. "Not directly, anyway. There's a rule about aiding and abetting denizens of Satan's realm. We'd be thrown down from above. And from what I've heard, that's an unpleasant experience."

"Probably don't compare with five minutes in Hell," Frank muttered. "So, what *can* you do?"

"We are authorized to engage and destroy all souls that have escaped from the Dark One's prison. Our orders are to shoot to kill. Well, to destroy. I'm sure you're packing some of those nifty green bullets?"

Frank nodded.

"We have something similar."

"So, why haven't you destroyed these prisoners yet?" Spike tipped his hat back as he asked.

"We can't."

"You can't?" Frank's irritation rose a notch.

"They still occupy the bodies of living mortals. We can't harm those from this world. We can advise the living, and protect them, but we cannot harm them. Only people from yours."

"Technically," said Corbett, "we shouldn't even be talking to you. You're evil—we're supposed to shoot you on sight."

"So, let me get this straight." Camille ran a finger along the handle of her knife as she shoved forward.

CHRIS BARILI

"You can't help us. You can't be seen with us. What you *can* do, though, is destroy us? I don't see this relationship as good for anyone."

Frank eased her back with a hand on her shoulder. She shot him a glare as frigid as the air outside. Then she shook her head and turned away.

"You're gonna get us all killed."

"You're already dead." Corbett frowned. "We all are, except those two."

He pointed at Stan and Curtis.

Camille wheeled again and tried to rush him, but Frank stepped in front of her, blocking her path. She faced off with him a moment, blue eyes flashing. Her breath came in torrents, as if her rage was tearing at her insides in an attempt to get out.

"Some of us want to stay in this world." She growled over Frank's shoulder at the two men in gray. "We have unfinished business here, and one of your special bullets would keep us from it."

"Such business is best left undone." Concern tinged Mills' voice, and he looked at her like a father might look at an injured child. "But if you're worried about it, you have my word that we will not harm you so long as you don't interfere with our work."

She whirled away and Frank faced Mills. "Agreed. Seems to me we can help one another out. We can shoot those people Booth and his men have possessed, and any others they might control. And you've done the detective work already. What have you found out?"

The tension in the room relaxed a notch as Camille walked to the French doors and stared out into the night, while the others sat on chairs, on the bed, or leaned against the door. Only Frank and Mills stood.

"We believe Booth is after more than just Lucy

Chandler." The detective paced as he talked, as if reasoning things through in his head. "But he definitely wants to have her for his own, too. So, if we can snatch her from his little gang, that might make him angry enough to make a mistake or two."

Frank scratched his chin. "Is he still here in Newport?"

"At the Aquidneck House Hotel," Mills answered. "Just a few doors from here. Whole gang, last we checked."

"Well, let's go round 'em up."

"Not so fast there, Marshal." Mills started to put his hand out to stop him, but a glare from Frank stopped him short. He cleared his throat. "We have reason to believe Mrs. Chandler is in there with them. If we storm the place, they could hurt her, and we have orders—"

Frank cut him off. "To minimize casualties to the living."

Mills nodded.

Stan straightened against the door. "What makes you think he's up to more than just taking back the love of his life?"

"We know that the people Booth and his gang have...occupied visited several establishments in Newport, as well as in Virginia, D.C., and Maryland known to house confederate sympathizers."

"This late?" Frank asked. "It's over two decades since the war ended. They haven't given up yet?"

Corbett shook his head. "Confederate sympathizers exist all over the south, and are even common in the capitol area. Occasionally, you'll see a rebel flag in someone's barn or bunkhouse. People don't let go of their dreams easy, even if the dream proves stupid.

"At first, we thought they might be going after the

remaining members of Lincoln's cabinet from 1865. Their conspiracy called for them to kill Lincoln as well as the Vice President and Secretary of State, but they failed on the last two."

Mills studied a Bible on the table, running a finger over its cover like it was something he'd lost. "George Atzerodt was supposed to kill the Vice, but turned yellow and got drunk instead. Lewis Powell was sent to dispatch the Secretary of State, but failed to kill him."

"So, that's it, then." Spike scratched his head. "We find those men and protect them. When Booth and his fellow escapees show up, we send 'em back to eternal fire and all go on our way."

Corbett shook his head. "Vice President Johnson and Secretary Seward both died years ago."

Frank knuckled his forehead. "Then, it must be Lucy," he reasoned. "And even if there is some larger plan here, we know they have her. We need her back and safe for either team to win this. So, let's go get her out."

"There is one small problem." Mills shifted from one foot to the other. Frank noticed both he and Corbett were touching the floor now. "He's surrounded the hotel with armed men, all living ones controlled by him and his gang. You'll have to fight your way in, and the instant they hear you coming, they'll kill her."

Frank concentrated, thinking over everything he'd heard.

"Can you two get inside without being seen?"

Corbett and Mills nodded.

"And once you're in there," Frank pressed, "you can keep Lucy alive?"

More nods.

"Then I have a plan.

CHAPTER SIX

Snow fell on Pelham Street, dusting the stones and making Frank slip as he shuffled toward the white four-story Aquidneck House Hotel. His muscles stiffened as he walked through the cold, moist air, and his left knee creaked with every step, the only sound seemingly not muffled by the blanket of white.

The rest of his crew fanned out behind him, except for Curtis, who'd been left in the room, much to the boy's disgruntlement. Camille trailed just behind Frank's left shoulder, Bowie gleaming green in her hand, while Spike followed behind his right. Batcho stalked through the darkness to their right, little more than a shadow slipping through night. They'd left Stan back at the park so he could use his glowing eyes and Sharps carbine to pick off any threats the group missed.

As they neared the hotel, men starting funneling out the front door, lining up on the porch, staring straight ahead, expressions blank. Frank recalled the last time they'd faced a group like this, outside a women's college in Liberty, Missouri. He'd nearly lost Camille that night, putting a bullet through her throat to save her from having her soul wiped from the universe.

He glanced back at the blonde, hoping to see some nostalgia from her, but her eyes focused on the hotel, expression grim.

Men had filed out onto the second-floor balconies now, too, and all of them, at once, raised rifles to their shoulders.

Frank drew his Colt, wiggling his trigger finger to work out its cold rigidity.

His gut tightened. These men were innocents, dragged into this battle by Booth and his men. They didn't deserve to die, and Frank didn't want to kill them.

As if they'd read his thoughts, the men around the hotel opened fire. A bullet tore into Frank's shoulder, rocking him back, but registering little pain. The first few never did hurt much, Frank remembered, and he unleashed a volley of forty-five caliber slugs at the porch, dropping at least two men.

Camille streaked past him, Bowie knife flashing as she jumped the porch rail and drove the blade hilt-deep into a man's skull. Spike opened fire on the right, and behind them, the Sharps rang out. A man fell from the balcony, hitting the street with a *whump*. Batcho streaked over the body, clearing the porch railing and driving another shooter to his knees.

Lead whizzed and cracked through the air around him as Frank fired and fired, fanning the hammer with barely enough time to aim. He killed two more before a slug took him in the thigh. This time, pain fired up his leg and into his hip.

Letting out a growl, Frank mowed down the man who'd fired the shot, and opened up on one of the balconies, killing two more. His heart broke with every shot, and tears froze on his cheeks.

So much death. For an instant, images from his dream flashed in his mind, but he forced them away and kept shooting.

Killing became as natural as breathing, his hand a blur on the hammer of his Colt. Needing an escape, Frank let himself become death, forgetting about his comrades and descending into the deep night of murder. He fired and fired until blood started to seep from his left hand, where it fanned the hammer. Bodies fell at an alarming rate, but he didn't care. He'd been born to do this. He was a gunfighter. A butcher.

"Frank!" Camille's voice seemed distant and muffled, like she was calling through a long tunnel. "Frank, stop!"

He ignored her, spraying round after round at the hotel. All he saw were targets falling, men dying. He needed nothing else.

Then, something careened into him, a snarling ball of teeth and fur, knocking him off his feet. He landed hard on the street, dropping the Colt and sliding through the snow. When he stopped, he flailed madly for his pistol, but Batcho put his paws on Frank's chest and the huge coyote pinned him to the ground. His yellow eyes glared down, and his lips peeled back to reveal their greenish glow. For an instant, Frank thought the coyote would rip his throat out. Instead, Batcho stepped off him and sat a few feet away, still snarling.

"Frank, it's over." Camille stood above him, brow

furrowed, while Spike offered a hand to help Frank to his feet. "They just…stopped shooting."

Sure enough, the few men still standing on the porch and balconies had dropped their weapons and stood stock-still as snow piled up on their shoulders and heads. Blood covered the hotel in spatters and sprays, and bodies littered the ground.

Frank let Spike pull him to his feet. He looked at his pistol where it lay in the snow and a chill ran down his spine.

"You all right, Marshal?" Spike asked.

"Buzzy warned me. This gun can consume me."

He picked up the pistol like it was a rattler, holding it at arm's length before dropping it into the holster.

Mills appeared in a third-story window and waved down to them, gray bowler in his hand. "We got her. Room 323."

Frank's muscles started to loosen up as soon as he entered the almost-vacant common room on the first floor. Several of the men with rifles milled about or sat at the white linen-covered tables, one staring down at his gun like he'd never seen it before. A fire roared in the fireplace against the back wall, and electric bulbs gave the room a warm glow. One serving girl stood near the fireplace, face pale, and tried not to look at Frank's group as they marched through her dining room.

Climbing the stairs to the third floor helped Frank limber up even more, and by the time they reached room 323, he felt almost like his old self. Well, his old dead self.

The room wasn't fancy, but the bed looked comfortable in its flower-patterned comforter and overstuffed feather pillows. A canopy nearly touched the ceiling, and striped wallpaper stretched from the hardwood floor to the tray ceiling. A handsome woman with brown ringlets and a strong jaw sat on the bed, hands in her lap.

Mills and Corbett stood beside a thin man seated in a wooden chair, his long fingers drumming and his eyes darting from Frank to each of his companions. His blond hair looked like squirrels lived there, and his narrow eyes made him look suspicious. He wore a simple white shirt and black vest, out of place among all the east coast finery.

"Frank, this here's the body of Mr. Stephen Hammond." Mills put a hand just above the man's shoulder, not quite touching it. "But Stephen's gone now, and this body's been possessed by George Atzerodt. George, meet Hell's Marshal. He's come to take you back."

Frank moved to stand in front of the seated man, making him tremble.

Hammond's eyes were a pale blue, almost gray like an overcast sky, but Frank saw fear behind them. Fear that belonged to Atzerodt.

"Don't make me go back." Hammond's voice shook and contained the hardened edges of a German accent, also Atzerodt's. "Booth made me follow him here. I didn't want to come. They'll punish me something fierce if I go back."

"Well, I reckon that'll depend on how much you cooperate with us. You help us, and maybe we can help you."

Atzerodt nodded a bit too eagerly for Frank's liking.

He turned to the lady on the couch.

"Mrs. Chandler?"

She nodded, her expression distant and nervous, like a bird trapped between two cats.

Mills stood beside Frank. "She's shaken."

Frank leaned over and peered into her blue eyes. She looked away and wrinkled her nose. Frank became keenly aware of his smell and how his appearance looked up close, so he rose.

"She's seen troubling things. She might never recover from this."

Stan stepped into the room. "I might be able to help with that."

He pushed his way to the bed and sat beside Lucy Chandler. She didn't seem as frightened of him as she had been of Frank, and actually met his gaze.

"He brought me here." Her voice was deep but shaking. "This is where we ended our engagement, and his letter was so…detailed. I thought it surely must have been him. But it wasn't at all. It was another man with his voice."

As she rambled, Stan started to mumble, the fingers on his hands dancing just below Lucy's vision. His movements quickened as she talked, until finally, he tapped his index finger in the middle of her forehead. Her eyes fluttered for a moment, then he eased her back on the bed.

"I'll take her home. When she wakes up, she won't remember any of this."

Corbett muttered something under his breath, and crossed himself.

"Dark magic," Mills said. "She will live with its taint the rest of her days."

Stan shrugged. "She'd have lived with the memories otherwise."

Satisfied, Frank turned to Hammond and crossed his arms over his chest.

"Time for you to start talking."

"I don't know anything," Atzerodt's German accent became heavier as his nerves wound tighter. "Booth, he wouldn't tell me his plans. Please, don't send me back!"

Frank nodded at Camille, and in a flash, her Bowie knife was at Atzerodt's throat. The eerie green dripped onto the nape of his neck.

"I'm sure you're familiar with that green stuff." Frank kept his voice low. "If she cuts you with that blade, your miserable soul will trot through your personal underworld before landing right back in Satan's living room. I don't think you want that, so start talking."

Atzerodt's eyes strained down, trying to keep Camille's blade in sight, then skipped from Frank to Mills and back to the Bowie.

"But, he's an angel, right? If I talk, can't he forgive me?"

Mills turned a stern gaze on the frightened man. "I ain't no angel, and only the Head Honcho can forgive you anyway. And I don't think he'll be much inclined toward helping you. But Marshal Butcher, here, he can always choose to leave your soul in this body, at least for now. He doesn't play by Heaven's rules like I do."

Atzerodt studied Frank's face for a moment, then hung his head and sobbed softly.

"Booth really didn't tell me much. He told me since I turned yellow last time—when I was supposed to kill the Vice President—that I could not be trusted with anything important this time. So, he brought me here and told me to delay you folks as long as I could.

"'Buy me time, George,' he told me. 'Slow down this marshal and his dead friends so the rest of us can complete our plans.' He told me to kill you if I could, but to at least buy him some time. I did that, didn't I?"

"So, this is a diversion," Frank muttered. "And we

walked right into it."

"Think harder," Camille pressed, pushing the blade harder against his skin. "What else? Did you overhear anything?"

His eyes watered, and he sniffled, like a child caught in a lie.

"Booth was talking to the others last night. He mentioned the Surratt House."

"What's that?"

"It's a tavern in Surrattsville, south of Washington. It's where we hid some carbines during the assassination. Mary Surratt is with Booth now, and her son still owns the place. Booth said they would get guns there. Lots of them. Enough for a small army."

"What do they need guns for?" Frank leaned down closer to the man and brushed the tip of his finger along the dull back side of Camille's Bowie. "Since Lucy here was obviously a distraction."

Atzerodt paled and eyed Camille's blade.

"I promise, they didn't tell me anything. Just that I needed to tie up Hell's posse for as long as possible."

"And what about us?" Mills asked, keeping his distance, as if he might get dirty if he got too close. "What did they tell you about angels?"

"He don't know you're coming. Or at least, he didn't tell us if he did."

Mills glanced at Frank. "That could give us an element of surprise."

"Did they tell you what to do if you survived this and killed us?" Frank asked.

Atzerodt hesitated. It wasn't much—just a quiver of his lip. Most people would have missed it. But Frank wasn't most people.

"Come on, 'fess up." He leaned closer and grinned as

Camille drew the blade down the other man's neck, across his chest, stopping on his breast bone. "You don't want my friend here to get impatient."

Atzerodt's lip shook again, and he nodded. "They told me to meet them at a hotel in Baltimore. Said they'd wait for me there until tomorrow, then move on without me."

"Which hotel?" Camille's voice sounded like violence restrained.

Atzerodt looked puzzled for a moment, then his eyes opened and he reached into his vest pocket. He fished around for a moment, then pulled out a brass key on a wooden tab. He handed it to Frank.

"This one."

Frank rose and Camille backed off. The wooden tab read, "Barnum City Hotel" on one side, and the number "601" on the other.

"Looks like we know where to find the gang now," he told the others. "That just leaves this."

He drew his pistol, chambered a Holy Water round with a mere thought, and shot Atzerodt in the forehead. The man's head snapped back and he toppled to the floor.

Mills jumped, and Camille's hand flew to her mouth.

A blanket of green light swirled around Hammond's body for a moment, then fled through the ceiling with an agonized scream.

Spike looked down at the man's still body and the blood spattered on the bed's fine cotton comforter. "But, he did what you asked."

"Orders are orders," Frank told him. "We're here to send all of these men back to Hell. Unless you'd like to fail this mission and go back yourself?"

Mills cleared his throat and pulled a folded blanket from the end of the bed to cover the corpse. "The authorities will respond soon to that gunshot. This isn't the wild west—they still take murder seriously here."

Frank looked at Mills. "You're the detective here. What do you think they're up to?"

Mills paced in front of the bed, scratching his chin. "Not sure, but it wasn't about his long-lost love."

"What was the goal of the Lincoln conspirators?" Stan asked. "What were they after, ultimately?"

"Southern victory," Corbett said. "Their original plot was to kidnap Lincoln and exchange him for confederate prisoners, but when that fell through, he decided killing Lincoln and the next two men in line would decapitate the Union and give the Confederacy a chance to rise up. He hated that Lincoln freed the slaves. Thought it was immoral."

"But that doesn't make much sense now," Frank added. "War's over. Rebels are hiding."

Mills shrugged. "Well, it sounds like he has enough firepower to do something big. I suppose it's possible he has enough soldiers to cause some trouble here."

Before anyone else could talk, Curtis burst into the room, panting as if he'd run up all the stairs to get to them.

"Boy, I told you to stay at the room!" Frank put his hands on his hips and glared down at the boy, but Curtis didn't blink.

"The local police are on the way. They're staging at our hotel. A dozen of them. You have about five minutes."

Stan moved first, lifting Lucy's still form and carrying her out the door.

"I'll get her home," he promised. "Meet you at the

hotel."

Mills and Corbett went to the window, sliding it open.

"We'll meet you back there, too." Both of them stepped out the window and strode away on thin air.

Camille and Spike moved to the door, but a newspaper on the table caught Frank's eye. The front page headline shouted, "Former President Hayes Dies."

Frank left the paper on the table and the three of them fled down the back stairs and out into the street.

CHAPTER SEVEN

Stan ran his team through the night, the stagecoach ripping down the eastern seaboard, passing New York City and Philadelphia so fast, the cities were little more than streaks of light. If anyone saw the coach or its ghastly passengers, no one said anything or tried to stop them.

When the sun peeked over the horizon to their left, Stan slowed and moved them at a more normal pace. Only Spike rode with the driver now, the others piled into the coach area so close that Camille had to sit with her thigh brushing Frank's, something that made him fight a grin, and her a scowl. They all huddled under thick blankets, but their dead bodies produced so little heat, they still stiffened miserably.

As they slowed, Frank stuck his head out the

window. Frost twinkled on pines and barren oaks, glittering like jewels in the rising sun, almost blinding him.

"We're about an hour north of Baltimore," Stan shouted back from the bench. His nose had turned cherry red, but he looked otherwise warm, despite wearing only his overcoat. "I'll take it slower here. Don't want to draw attention."

Mills touched Frank's shoulder. "Let's get out and walk a ways, Frank. I'd like a private word or two with you."

An intensity in the man's eyes made Frank nod and open the door.

"Hold up, Stan," he yelled. "Me and Mills are gonna hoof it."

They walked behind the carriage, allowing it to gain some distance from them. Frank shuffled like a ninety-year-old man for a few yards. But movement and the sun's warmth loosened his muscles until he strolled almost normally. Under their feet, frost crunched, and the morning air tasted like ice.

"Well, get around to it," Frank muttered. "Say your bit."

Mills studied him sidelong for a moment, then sighed and gazed off after the coach.

"I've spoken with your boy."

Frank stopped in his tracks, jaw falling open. A chasm seemed to open in his chest, letting the winter air in.

"You talked to Ron?"

Mills nodded. "I could get in a heap of trouble for this, but he wanted me to give you a message."

Frank forced himself to take a step. Then one more, and another, until he walked beside the detective again.

He struggled for words, his mouth emitting a spoonful of slop even he couldn't understand.

"You're shocked." Mills made as if to pat his shoulder in comfort, pausing just short of touching him. "But he sought me out. He wants you to know he forgives you. He wants you to know you it ain't your fault, all this killin'. You're just a puppet, dancing when your strings get pulled. You can forgive yourself."

"Then, why didn't he tell me himself?"

Mills shrugged. "It doesn't work that way. He's an angel, Frank. One of God's soldiers, and a dang good one. He's forbidden from contacting denizens of Hell, and even if he wasn't, contact from Heaven direct to Hell isn't possible. He'd have to send a messenger, and that would likely get him caught. We're tracked pretty close."

Frank thought of the dream. Was it a message from Ron? "He sent you."

"I was already coming. No skin off anyone's nose."

"He spoke to me here last time."

Mills raised his eyebrows. "That's…unusual, but in the living world, it's easier. There are fewer barriers between here and the Head Honcho's ranch. Certain things can be circumvented. It's even easier in the underworld, though. That's where the two ranches share a fence-line."

Frank turned that over in his mind. If he wanted to talk to Ron, the underworld was the best place to do it. Maybe next time he went to Buzzy's place, he could find a way.

"You gotta fix your head, Frank. Look at yourself— you're messier than a tumbleweed. You keep blaming yourself for everything. For Ron. For me. For all those people. But you're being controlled, and the only way to break that control is to forgive yourself."

Frank looked at the frost-covered tips of his boots as he walked. While his limbs were loosening, the nip in the air reminded him it was still winter in New England. He flexed his hands, wishing his gun fingers would loosen faster. No telling what they'd run into in pursuit of Booth and his gang.

"It ain't that easy." He didn't look at the detective, keeping his gaze down.

"I think it is. Those judges, they might not be the straightest shooters in Heaven or even Hell, but they know their jobs. If they tried to send you up, that's where you belong. Period.

"Get past what you did during your life and get to putting things right for eternity."

Before Frank could respond, the stage coach stopped ahead of them, maybe fifty yards further on. Stan looked back over his shoulder, put his fingers to his mouth, and whistled, a shrill sound that sliced through the crisp morning air like a sunbeam.

Mills and Frank jogged the rest of the way and found Stan had stopped at a fork in the dirt road, Hell's steeds huffing and clawing at the ground with their hoofs.

"What's the delay, Stan?" Frank patted the side of the coach with his hand, leaving a glove print in the frost formed there.

"We need to know where we're going now, Marshal. Which means we need to know what Booth is doing."

The group clambered down from the stage and stood in a circle, stretching and blowing into their hands. Spike stomped his feet, and Camille shrugged a thick, fur-lined stole around her shoulders.

"I've been thinking about that." Frank was glad for the distraction from his conversation with Mills. "Seems like we can't take any chances, and we can't waste any time. We need to check out both this Barnum City Hotel and the Surratt House at the same time."

"Then, this fork is the key," Stan told them. "One group can take the left fork and walk into Baltimore, about a half-day's travel south. The rest can ride in the stage on the right fork. It circles around the city and ends up heading south, toward Clinton. We should get there about the same time the other group reaches Baltimore."

A carriage trundled around a bed on the left fork, two horses the color of night snorting steam as they lugged an enclosed coach behind them. Stan moved his stage off the road to let them pass, keeping his demon-mounts quiet. But the normal horses picked up on something, probably the stink of death, and tossed their heads, whinnying nervously. The other driver eyed Frank's group with suspicion, but moved along.

When the other carriage was out of earshot, Stan spoke.

"Might be hard to blend in around these parts. We all stand out a good bit from these fine folks."

Frank stared down the left fork, and nodded. "Then, we'd best get things moving. I hope Booth still thinks we're delayed up in Newport."

"Not likely," Mills said. "He's been one step ahead of us this whole time, leading us where he wants us to go."

"Then, we'll have to be smarter." Frank pointed down the right fork. "Stan, take Spike and Curtis around the city and check out the Surratt House in Clinton. See if that weapons cache is still there. If it is, watch the place until we get there. Take our angelic friends with you, too. You're more likely to run into trouble with all those guns, I suspect."

Mills shook his head, and beside him, Corbett

shifted his stance.

"We're heading to the capitol," the one-time detective announced. "Your people are more than enough to handle these tasks. Sergeant Corbett and I will see what we can figure out in D.C. and if we find something, we'll meet you in Clinton tonight. Tomorrow morning at the latest."

Frank hesitated. He really wanted the extra people with Curtis, but it wasn't like Mills and Corbett could do much anyway.

He nodded. "Then, Camille and I will head into Baltimore and check out this Barnum City Hotel. See what we can find. We'll all meet up in Clinton by tomorrow morning."

Everyone nodded, and Frank started off down the left fork, Camille falling in at his side. Stan's coach rattled off down the right fork, the driver cracking his whip. To Frank's surprise, Batcho slipped into the trees along the left fork and paralleled their track.

"Looks like we get the coyote," Frank told Camille.

She narrowed her eyes at the shadowy form as it slipped through the woods.

"Not sure that makes me feel any better."

Frank had to agree.

CHAPTER EIGHT

Frank and Camille hit the outskirts of Baltimore as night lowered a purplish-black curtain across the city, bringing with it a damp, biting cold. It stabbed through their coats and made it feel as if their clothing had been soaked to the skin.

Frank's muscles stiffened as he shuffled down North Calvert Street, the brick and stone buildings rising up stories above the street, their windows lit like eyes keeping watch over the people below. There weren't many folks out and about, though, as winter had driven most to the warmth of their living rooms or beds.

"Map says the hotel's at the corner with Fay-yeti," Frank grumbled, stomping his feet to drive feeling back into his toes.

"Fayette," Camille corrected. "It's French."

Frank shrugged. "Oughta be American, especially out here, where the country was born."

She groaned and shook her head.

Behind them, hidden somewhere in the shadows, Batcho growled. Frank could almost feel the animal's tension, his own hackles rising a bit at the sound of his snarl.

"He's scared of something," he told Camille. "It takes a lot to scare that coyote, too."

"We know what scares him most. Means we're being followed by someone that came from the same place we did."

"Or something."

Frank let that thought hang in the air between them, and Camille slipped her hands through his elbow.

"Do you think it's another Hellhound?"

Frank shook his head. "Hellhounds would have hit us by now."

"Great. We're in a strange city being followed by some strange creature from Hell and the rest of our group isn't even in town to help us."

"And we're not there to help them, either, if they're being followed."

That silenced her, and Frank knew her thoughts had skipped to Curtis. They'd all grown fond of the little con artist, forming an odd kind of family with him. Something none of them had known before.

They reached Barnum City Hotel a few minutes later, both of them stiff and numb, but neither willing to take the first steps into the massive brick and stone building. It hulked before them like a fortress, cold and hard, seemingly impregnable. Even the yellow light coming from most windows seemed chilled, as if something had sucked the warmth from it.

"You ready for what we might find inside?" Frank loosened his pistol in its holster. "Booth has been one step ahead of us at every stop. He's likely to ambush us at some point."

Camille drew her Bowie and held its glowing green blade up in front of her face.

"We're already dead." Her voice was cold as the night. "We've faced hordes of dead, Hellhounds, and worse. We can handle whatever's in here."

Frank studied her cool expression, and for a moment, he feared for Booth — or whoever they found inside.

"Then, let's get it done." He moved off toward the hotel.

The granite front steps led up to a front porch ringed with columns of white. Frank stopped and stared up at the six stories above him. Balconies stood empty at every other window, and the upper floors seemed to disappear into the night sky, as if existing in a different world. Suddenly, room 601 seemed like it sat at the peak of a mountain shrouded in snow and ice.

Camille strode up the stairs and in the front door, leaving Frank to keep up.

For all the frigid cold outside, the lobby of the Barnum City Hotel glowed with light and warmth, dozens of lamps and chandeliers basking the room in heat. The black-and-white marble floor shone and made their heels clack loudly as they marched past the stuffy-looking bellhop toward a set of stairs at the back. Well-cultured guests in suits and dresses parted for them as if afraid they might catch something. Before they reached the steps, a busybody manager in a white shirt and dress vest intercepted them. His slicked back hair shone like the floor, and he looked down his slender nose at Frank.

"May I help you…sir?"

Frank was about to tell him to get the Hell out of the way when Camille interrupted.

"We're just going to our room. 601."

The manager raised his over-sculpted eyebrows, so Frank dangled the key in front of his face.

"See. 601."

The stuffy little man looked up at Frank with an expression bordering on insolence until he met Frank's gaze. Something about Frank must have made an impression, for the manager sniffed, looked at the floor, and motioned up the stairs.

"My apologies. We can't be too careful with the presidential suites."

As Frank climbed the steps behind Camille, he was pretty sure he felt the manager's gaze drilling holes in his back.

The ascent served to loosen the rigid muscles in his back and legs, and by the time they reached the sixth floor, Frank felt almost alive again. Almost.

Room 601's door stood slightly ajar, and the light spilling out made Frank's gut clench. He drew his Colt and pressed himself against the wall to the right of the door. Camille flattened against the left, blade glowing ghastly green.

"I don't hear anything," she said.

Frank listened a moment, then nodded. Standing back, he nudged the door open with the toe of his boot. He swept the room, gaze and pistol in perfect unison as they moved from right to left. The room was a mess, bedsheets tossed on the floor, open bottles of whiskey and rye on a cherry wood table. A chair lay tipped on its back on an expensive-looking rug that had been stained with foul-smelling tobacco wads.

"Looks like they left in a hurry." Camille re-sheathed her Bowie and took a hesitant step inside. "And I'm guessing they didn't pay their bill."

Frank followed her in, but held onto his pistol for the time being. As he crossed the threshold, something tingled on his skin, like he'd been standing in the open during a thunderstorm. Then, the feeling disappeared as suddenly as it had started.

"They were supposed to meet their man here, so where are they?"

"Unless they lied to him about that too."

"So they could mislead us. Send us in the wrong direction."

She nodded and moved to the table, picking up a newspaper. She held it up for Frank to see.

Someone had circled in ink a headline that read, "President Hayes' Funeral Procession."

"Says here the Hayes will be buried on the twentieth," Camille noted. "That's tomorrow. In Fremont, Ohio. Says it's a state funeral. Don't presidents attend those?"

Frank nodded, unconvinced. His gut told him something was off.

"Seems too easy, but what else do we have?"

She dropped the paper and picked up a paper box. "An empty bullet box." She held it up. "Forty-one caliber."

Outside, Batcho howled. Frank and Camille exchanged a glance, and ran to the tall, curtained window. There, in the street six stories down, stood the coyote, looking up at them as if he knew exactly where they were. Onlookers gave him a wide berth, several scrambling for the safety of the lobby.

Batcho tipped his head back and howled again,

finishing with a snarl and a show of teeth at the shadows to his left.

"Better see what he's up to," Frank said.

He took the steps down in a hurry, Camille keeping pace right behind him. They bounded down the last flight, into the lobby, only to come face-to-face with the same manager.

"Pardon me...sir." He wrinkled his nose and Frank wondered if his body had started to stink in the warm, inside air. "You have a call."

"What?"

The thin little man cleared his throat and pointed at the lobby desk.

"A call. On the telephone."

Frank looked at Camille, but the hooker shrugged and shook her head. With a roll of his eyes, the manager led them the desk and picked up a curved, black handle-like device, with a cup at one end and a disk at the other. A wire connected it to a box on the desk.

"It's a telephone." He peered down his slim nose. "Surely you've heard of them?"

Frank shook his head and forced his hand to grasp it like it was a venomous snake.

"You listen here." The manager pointed to the disk. "And speak into this."

He pointed to the other end.

Frank held the listening end a few inches from his head, making the manager sigh with exasperation and nudge it until it touched Frank's ear.

"Say something."

"Uh, yes?"

The voice on the other end sound distant and muffled, and was covered in crackles and pops, but Frank knew it as Stan right away.

"That you, Frank?"

Frank held the phone out, examined it, then returned it to his ear.

"Stan? Where are you?"

"We're in Clinton, Frank. Spike's here, and Curtis. Did you find anything?"

Frank wanted to drop the phone and step away, maybe even shoot it. He wondered if it was some sort of magic, like Stan's, but no one else in the crowded lobby seemed to even take note of him talking to the device. So, he kept talking, telling Stan what they'd found in the hotel room. When he finished, Stan muttered to someone on his end, then sighed.

"Mills says those bullets are the same caliber Booth used to kill Lincoln. His preferred weapon is a Derringer."

Frank scratched his chin on the phone. "Did you find anything?"

"Nothing. We got to the Surratt House, just like Atzerodt said, but it was empty. No one was there, and nothing suspicious. But they did set a trap for us."

"What kind of trap?" A sinking feeling twisted Frank's gut.

"A kind of a magical tripwire. Designed to alert someone — or something — to our presence. Fortunately, I sensed it before we set it off or we might have been ambushed."

The tingling feeling. Batcho's odd behavior. Suddenly, Frank knew what his gut had been trying to tell him.

"Get to Ohio as fast as you can. This is our best chance to get Booth and his people. We know where they're going to be. If we're not there, do what you can with Mills' help."

"Frank—"

"We have to go, Stan. We tripped a wire on this end, and something's coming for us."

He handed the phone to the manager, who took it with two fingers, as if it were covered in blood. Gingerly, he set it back in its cradle.

"Who's president right now?" Frank asked.

"Benjamin Harrison," the manager replied, not hiding his disdain for his unwanted guests. "But only until Grover Cleveland takes office in March. Now, there's a good man! Why, Cleveland—"

Ignoring him, Frank took Camille by the elbow and led her out the door, onto the front steps.

Their breath steamed in front of their faces as they searched the empty street for signs of life, but the night seemed to have been frozen still. Frank's boots echoed throughout the street, even though he tried to tiptoe down the marble steps. Beside him, Camille cringed with every footfall, hand locked on the handle of her Bowie.

No sooner did they reach the open expanse of street below than a shadow detached itself from the darkness and barred their path.

CHAPTER NINE

Before them stood a diminutive woman, dressed in stiff, black wool, hair curled under just above her shoulders. Her mouth had been drawn into a thin line, and she glared at them with eyes as dark as the alley behind her.

"I see that coward George failed to stop you."

"Mary Surratt, I assume?" Frank put his hand on his six-shooter.

"In spirit only." Her voice was hard-edged, like a stone knife. "I borrowed this body from a woman who just happened to look like me. She's a good bit smaller than I was, but in the end, that won't matter."

Camille stepped forward, drawing her knife. The blade cast green light across her face.

"I'll handle this one."

Surratt laughed, a dry, scraping sound, like a casket

lid sliding open.

"You think because I'm a woman, you're the one that should fight me? You're a fool. It's not me you'll be fighting."

She raised her hands from her sides, palms up, and dropped her chin to her chest. As she did, three more figures emerged and stood behind her.

At least part human, there were two men and one woman, and not unattractive ones at that. The men stood at least six feet tall, rippling with muscle and sinew, clad only in the shredded remains of trousers. The woman wasn't much shorter, and equally chiseled, with breasts every bit as muscular as the rest of her. Ram's horns sprouted from their heads, curling around their ears to form bony helmets, and leathery wings sprouted from their backs, unfurling as they took their places beside Mary Surratt.

Their eyes smoldered red, as if embers had been pushed into their sockets.

Frank snapped his jaw shut, and Camille stepped back beside him, uncertainty sweeping her confidence away.

"I'm betting you've never heard of cambions." Surratt's voice cracked through the night like an axe through wood. "These little beasties were born when certain demons bred with humans, so they share the power of a demon with the intelligence of a human. Normally, they'd tear this body of mine apart, but these ones have been...persuaded to take orders from me instead."

She raised her head and stared Frank in the eye with her cold, midnight gaze.

"And I ordered them to destroy you."

The cambions moved so fast, Frank couldn't react

quickly enough to shoot them. They became blurs, streaking from their positions behind Surrat and dashing at Camille and Frank. Frank fired twice, but by the time his muzzle flashed both times, the beast was gone.

The males appeared beside Frank in a heartbeat, raking his torso with sharp claws. Pain lanced through his body, and he nearly dropped his Colt. He fired again and again, each time aiming just an instant too slow, the creature disappearing before the bullet could tear into it.

To his left, Camille slashed and stabbed, her blade carving green arcs through the night air, but as far as he could tell, she never drew blood. Not even once.

One of the males popped into existence in front of Frank, hammering him with his fists. Bones cracked as Frank sailed backward, just to be struck from behind by the other male. Frank's neck popped as he fell forward on his face, but he ignored the pain in his chest and rolled just as the second beast leapt for him.

Frank fired, and this time, his bullet ripped into the thing's chest with a flash of green light. If the creature felt it, he showed no sign, falling on Frank with arms flailing, claws bared. Frank fired again and again and again, his barrel against the thing's chest. Finally, it shrieked, threw back its head, and fell writhing to the street as green mist swirled around it like a dozen boa constrictors. Its flesh torched, green flames dancing across its skin, making it howl even louder as it tried in vain to beat the blaze out. An instant later, it turned to ash on the stones.

The second male crept backward, cautious now, hands raised. Frank ventured a glance at Camille in time to see her grapple with the female cambion. She raised her Bowie, driving it toward the beast's chest, but the cambion fought back, grasping her wrist in a clawed hand and holding it at bay.

Out the corner of his eye, Frank saw the second male move and he fired without looking. The bullet ripped into the thing's thigh, making a searing sound as it passed through flesh and bone. The cambion cried out, grasped at its thigh, and glared at Frank, eyes red with hate. Then, it beat its wings and flew off, into the night.

Frank rushed to Camille, who still struggled with the female, her knife no closer to the thing's ribs than it had been. Frank leveled the barrel of his pistol at the beast's skull and cocked the hammer back.

"I'll wager you saw what happened to your ugly friend."

The cambion stopped struggling, turning its gaze on Frank. For a moment—less than a heartbeat, really—Frank saw something else in those eyes, something softer. For a split second, the red disappeared and was replaced with the deep brown of human eyes. And in that same blink of an eye, he thought he saw fear.

He put his free hand on Camille's knife and eased it back from the cambion's chest. His strength was ebbing, his legs trembling and the tip of his pistol shook. He needed to rest. Rebuild his body.

"Get gone," he told the monster. "Don't look back."

Camille let go. The creature studied them for just a second, then took to flight. Frank watched it go as his strength gave out and he fell to his knees.

"Well, isn't that something?" Surratt said behind them. "Looks like I'll have to do this myself. Should've known I couldn't trust halflings."

And suddenly, she started to change.

Frank winced as the sound of bones snapping and flesh tearing shredded the night's silence. Mary Surratt—or the body she had possessed—doubled over, her back hunching as she dropped to all fours. She wailed in pain and rage as her body transformed, twisting and cracking, skin ripping open to allow dark, oily tufts of fur to erupt forth. Pointed ears emerged from her head, along with short, sharp-looking horns no longer than Frank's hand.

Her eyes took on a yellow glow, and a hairless, scaled tail twisted from her back end, whipping around her.

Frank forced himself to his feet and stepped back, knees wobbling, as he took in the horrific monster that now stood before him. Mary Surratt had become some sort of large cat, bigger than any cougar he'd ever seen. She let out a deathly growl, drool dripping from long fangs, and fixed him with her yellow cat eyes.

Camille circled to the creature's right, and Frank aimed at the cat's head with his Colt.

"Try and shoot me, gunfighter," the Surratt-thing mewled. "If you can."

Tattered wings sprouted from her back and she took to the air, hovering over the street.

If the cambions were fast, Surratt's new form was impossibly so. Where they'd been blurs, she simply seemed to appear in new places. Frank fired off six rounds, each one missing, before she finally popped up behind him and dug her fangs into his shoulder.

He expected fire to burn through him, but this time, it felt like her bite injected ice into his veins. His entire body went numb, and his limbs refused to move. His pistol dropped from his grip, and he tried to scream, but even his voice seemed frozen in his throat.

Then Camille was there, green blade flashing through the night, arcing toward the creature's eye. But the thing was too fast, swiping the hooker aside like she was a toy, sending her tumbling to lay still on the cobblestones.

Frank closed his eyes as the Surratt-thing drove him to the street, freeing her jaws of his shoulder, but putting razor-sharp claws on his back, each one piercing his dead flesh and sending pinpricks of ice into his lungs. He felt himself fading, knew that he'd lost. He wanted only to yell for Camille to run, but couldn't even muster the strength to do that.

He caught motion out the corner of his eye, and in a flash, something barreled into the creature with a snarl, knocking it off him and driving it back onto the hotel steps. Frank forced himself to his feet to see Batcho facing off with Surratt, the two circling each other like predators.

Batcho looked like a mere puppy compared to the massive cat before him, but he growled and bared his teeth, crouched and ready to spring at the thing's throat. Green slobber dripped from his maw.

Frank grabbed his pistol and crawled to Camille's side. She woke, shaking her head and rubbing at her neck, but brushed his hands away when he tried to help her sit.

Batcho glanced back over his shoulder at them, then tilted his head back and howled, a soulful, mourning sound that echoed through the streets like a funeral dirge.

"He wants us to run." Camille pushed to her feet. "Come on, we need to go."

Frank fought to stand, aiming his gun at the cat-thing.

"We can't just leave him."

And just like that, the two creatures crashed together, a mass of fur and teeth, blood and bone, whirling and biting and clawing at one another so fast, Frank couldn't keep up. Green splashed through the air, stark against the red of blood.

"We can't beat that thing," Camille cried. "He's buying us time, Frank. We need to run!"

Pulling his elbow, she started toward an alley on their left. Frank resisted, transfixed on the battle. The coyote was losing—that was obvious. He bled from a dozen wounds, and his attacks were becoming less and less fierce. Even the green in his fangs seemed weaker. But still Batcho fought, letting out another despairing howl.

"Gunfighter, now!" Camille kicked him in the leg, and that was enough.

Taking one last look at his friend and guide, Frank sprinted for the alley. As he rounded the corner, Batcho yelped in agony, then fell silent.

CHAPTER TEN

Frank fired, his left hand a blur as it fanned the hammer on his Colt, fire blazing from the barrel. Before him, blood flew and men fell. Good men, innocent men, in uniforms gray and blue alike. Their blood flowed onto the scorched earth, pooling around his ankles, over the top of his boots and soaking his socks.

He walked forward, a specter spitting fire from his hand, dealing out death like cards in a poker game. He'd become a killing machine, and while his victims fired back, lead whizzing past his ears and ripping through his body, he was unstoppable. Wherever he looked, men died.

His heart froze at the sight. He tried, through sheer strength of will, to stop the reaping, but he could no more stop himself than he could escape the river of blood that threatened to sweep him away.

"Frank, help me!" The voice slipped through death's wailing, a whisper among screams. "Hurry!"

Frank surged forward, sloshing through red, kicking waves of blood ahead of him as he cut down men left and right. He knew the voice, had heard it before, but he couldn't dig the memory from the depths of his mind.

"Frank, please!"

Frank stopped shooting, and his gaze swept the throng around him, searching for the source of the voice. It sounded like a child, high-pitched and shrill. And it pulled at the strings of his heart, tugging him forward as he cut his way through his enemies.

Then he saw him, a boy no older than ten, freckles dusted across his nose and cheeks as he struggled against two men, one holding each rail-thin arm. Behind him, a third man—this one in a charcoal duster—leveled a pistol at the boy's head. Red eyes glared out from under the figure's hat, twisting Frank's gut and tugging at his mind. Between Frank and the boy stood a hundred men and women, all armed, all waiting for Frank.

He knew that to save the boy, he had to shoot his way through the men and women. In fact, his gun had already come up, almost of its own accord. The figure behind the boy laughed.

Tears ran down the boy's cheeks, making his freckles sparkle like amethysts.

"Curtis." The name rushed to the front of his mind. "Curtis, hold on, son."

Frank strode forward, gun still smoking, eyes locked on the figure. The men and women between them raised their guns.

"You gotta kill 'em all, Frank!"

Frank stumbled and a rough, gravelly laugh hissed

from the figure. His eyes flared.

Frank's gun barrel dropped an inch. These were innocent people, men and women. Mothers and fathers. He couldn't—

"Marshal, you all right?" He knew the woman's voice, needed it, but lost it in the din around him.

Frank advanced one slow, inexorable step, his pistol half-raised, eyes sweeping across the faces of the people before him. One woman raised a shotgun and fired, the slug whizzing past his ear. Frank dropped her with a bullet between the eyes, and that was all it took.

Gunfire exploded in a series of cracks and pops and booms, lead ripping through Frank and zipping past him from all directions. Men and woman cried out as they died, dropping in droves, their voices a cacophony of dread, swirling around him.

His gun hand began to shake, the barrel wavering, shots going wide or high. The shadowy figure's eyes flared again, stabbing Frank's heart with their heat, and his hand steadied. He dropped his next two targets, then hesitated again.

The figure drew his pistol and pointed it at Frank

"Frank, wake up!" The woman's voice insisted now, pleaded.

"You're a killer." The figure's voice hissed through smoke-stained teeth as he pulled back the hammer on his gun. Green light swirled from the breach. "You'll never change. You'll keep killing as long as I need you to. And then, I'll destroy you."

The figure fired.

"Frank, wake up!"

Frank jolted awake to find Camille's face just an inch from his own, her blue eyes ringed with red. Dark half-moons hung under them where flesh had started to sag and slough. She gripped his shoulders like a frightened mother might grip a child.

"You need rest," he told her, taking in the clackity-clack of the train tracks slipping by underneath them. "You look like Hell."

She pulled back, irritation flitting across her face.

"Not like I could sleep with you babbling in your dreams," she complained, leaning against the deep brown leather of her seat. They were alone in the compartment, having frightened off a young couple earlier. "Besides, one of us had to keep watch."

Frank nodded and stretched, a yawn clawing its way out of him. He felt better, physically anyway, but the remnants of the dream still seemed real, haunting the back of his mind like a ghost in a shadowed attic.

The details of the dream nagged at him, whispering that he was a killer. Murderer. Butcher.

"How far are we?"

Camille shrugged. "You slept a couple hours, so we're probably in Pennsylvania somewhere."

At least they were still streaking west, hoping to catch Booth and his gang before they could assassinate the President. Frank knew their mission was to take him back to Hell, not save Benjamin Harrison, but if he let them succeed, it all seemed pointless.

He slid to the window on his right. He was facing the back of the train, and saw what they'd already passed as it streaked by outside. Trees, houses, poles with telegraph—or now, he supposed, telephone—wires between them. All turned to monotone blurs as he leaned his head against the cool glass.

"I'm gonna get some sleep," Camille told him.

Frank nodded and lifted his head off the window so he wouldn't be as likely to nod off. He needed Camille at her best, so she needed time to rest and rebuild as he had done.

Still, no sooner had she rested her head against her seatback than Frank felt a heavy pressure in his gut as he was pushed back a bit into his seat.

"What's happening?" Camille asked, suddenly alert. Her hand drifted toward the Bowie at her hip.

"We're speeding up."

"Why would a train suddenly speed up in the middle of nowhere?"

There was only one reason. "Robbers. They're gonna try to outrun 'em."

Camille vaulted to her feet. "Robbers? Out west, sure, but in Pennsylvania?"

Frank gazed out the window again as something appeared alongside the tracks near the end of the train. A black stagecoach raced up on them, easily passing car after car like the train was standing still. Frank knew the stage as soon as he saw it and pushed himself out of the seat.

"It's Stan."

The two of them left the compartment and shouldered their way down the narrow corridor of the passenger car. No one else seemed to have noticed the train's new speed, as the corridor remained vacant until the conductor stepped through a door at the front end.

A portly man, he waddled down the hall, waving his hands at Frank and Camille. Sweat beaded his forehead, despite the chill in the air. Spectacles perched high on his nose, looking like they were somehow stuck to his eyes.

"Please return to your compartment," he stammered, eyes darting to each of them. "We're being—"

"You ain't being robbed," Frank said. "Those are

friends of mine, and they just want the lady and me. Stop the train and we'll get off. They'll leave the rest of you alone."

The man shook his jowly head. "We at the Reading Company could never allow our passengers to sacrifice themselves for us. We will protect you. Besides, Captain James and his squad of Army soldiers will handle these bandits."

Camille and Frank exchanged a glance.

"Where are these soldiers?" Camille moved close to the conductor, jabbing his chest with a fingernail.

The man blanched and wrinkled his nose. "Box car right behind the engine."

"How many?"

The conductor's gaze flicked from Camille to Frank and back. "Ten. Maybe twelve. They're guarding a gold shipment for the Army."

With Camille close on his heels, Frank sprinted down the corridor, his long-dead muscles stretching and loosening from the cold and the sitting. He tossed doors aside like paper as he jumped from car to car, knocking one pompous-looking man in a suit backward into his compartment. The man started to protest, but got one look at Camille and thought better of it.

They burst into an open passenger car, with rows of seats rather than private compartments, drawing surprised stares from a dozen or so travelers. The rest kept their eyes fixed out the left windows, where Stan's ebony stage continued its race toward the front of the train.

"Hurry!" Frank yelled to Camille.

The next door opened to a box car, just as the conductor had said. Its rear door stood open, with a young soldier in the deep blue of an Army uniform leaning out, rifle trained on the encroaching stage.

He glanced at Frank and Camille. "Get back in the passenger car! We'll handle these bandits!"

"Those ain't bandits, soldier!" Frank grabbed the rifle and jerked it from the shocked man's hands. "They're our friends."

The soldier reached for his sidearm, a polished, blue six-shooter, and Frank froze. Images of his nightmare flashed in his mind, of soldiers dying. Good men fell in a lake of blood, and as the private's pistol came up, Frank found himself frozen. How many more innocent men would he have to kill?

The soldier aimed his pistol and pulled back the hammer. Frank still didn't move, couldn't. This man was doing his job, his duty even. He couldn't kill him.

Camille's Bowie flashed past him, embedding itself in the man's throat. He fell backward into the box car as gunshots rang out inside.

"They're shooting at the stage!" Camille shoved Frank in the back, urging him toward the box car full of soldiers. "Curtis is with him!"

Frank woke up, his mind suddenly alert.

"Try not to kill 'em," he shouted.

Then, wielding the rifle like a club, he leapt into the box car.

The soldiers froze for an instant, stunned at the sight of a man and a woman rushing them, but they were seasoned fighters, and their confusion didn't last long.

Frank dropped one with a rifle butt to the face, then knocked out a second with an overhand swing of the gun, clocking him on the temple. Camille drove the butt of her Bowie against a young corporal's jaw, shattering bone and teeth, then brought her knee up into the groin of a sergeant who made the mistake of grabbing her by the shoulders.

But their element of surprise wore off after that. A soldier drove his shoulder into Frank's back, knocking him to the floor, rifle skittering out of his hands. A second man fell on him, pummeling Frank's ribs with punch after punch. They didn't hurt, but Frank heard a rib snap, and knew he had to put an end to this now, before Stan and Curtis took more fire.

He boxed the soldier's ears, then gouged him in the eye, tossing the man aside like a pillow, and lurching to his feet. Across the car from him, two soldiers stood by the open side door. Stan's stage thundered along beside the train, Curtis on the seat between the car and Stan.

Both soldiers raised their rifles, and Stan wrapped his arm around Curtis, as if it could shield the boy from incoming bullets.

"Don't shoot!" Frank yelled.

Before they could fire, Camille careened into them from the side, knocking one man out the door. She managed to grab the handle, but dangled out the door herself, golden hair whipping around in the wind.

At the door, the second soldier aimed his carbine at Camille, but Frank had already cleared the gap. He slugged the man on his jaw, dropping him to the floor.

He hauled Camille back inside. The two fell to a heap on the cold floor, Camille on top of Frank. She looked into his eyes for a split second, and he thought he saw softness there, something less than the cold and ice he normally found.

Then, the moment passed and she rolled off him. She grabbed one of the downed soldiers by his hair, hauled him to his feet, and pressed the blade of her Bowie to his throat. The other soldiers — all struggling to their feet–froze in place.

Frank trained his Colt on them.

"One of you needs to stop this train," he growled. "We'll get off, and our friends will take us. You move on and never see us again."

"Or, at least, you'd better hope you don't," Camille added.

The sergeant stood, rubbing the back of his neck and started for the front of the car.

"I'll get the engineer to stop." He eyed Camille like she was an uncaged predator. "Just don't hurt him. You've already murdered two good men."

Frank winced, but kept his gun on them.

The sergeant slid the front end door open and waved over the coal tender car to the engineer, a soot-covered man with a bushy moustache. The engineer waved back, and with a hiss of steam, then train slowed. A few minutes later, they came to a stop in a stretch of woods, tall pine trees rising on either side of the train, Stan's stage tucked tightly against the coal car ahead of them as Frank climbed down to the ballast.

Curtis bolted from the stage, darting to Frank and wrapping his arms around Frank's waist. "I thought you were…"

Stan approached and stood, grinning, behind the boy. Spike waved from the coach's driver seat, a meaty hand almost blocking out the sun.

Frank tousled the boy's hair. "Takes more than a few cambion to kill me."

At mention of the half-breeds, Stan's expression darkened.

"Sounds like we have a lot to talk about on the way."

"On our way where?" Camille had dragged the soldier out of the car, still pressing her knife to his throat.

"Back to Washington. Mills paid us a visit. Looks

like Booth and his boys never left there."

"What about the President?" Frank wasn't completely surprised. Something had seemed off about their assumption anyway.

Stan shook his head. "Not going. Scarlet fever in the White House, so President Elect Cleveland is attending. Booth and his brood are back in D.C., and Mills thinks they're after President Harrison."

"Now things make sense. Booth hated that blacks got the right to vote, so Harrison is his logical choice. The man supported and promoted negroes voting."

"And he's the current president," Stan said. "Killing him would stagger the government, unlike killing his replacement."

"How much time do we have?"

"Not enough," Stan replied. Mills' source says tomorrow morning."

Frank nodded to Camille. "You can let him go now."

She shook her head. "That sergeant still looks a might bit angry. Let's let this one go once we're on our way."

She was right. The sergeant still glowered in the door to the rail car, and he'd picked up a rifle. He and several of his men looked ready to shoot Frank and his people where they stood.

"We'll release your friend here a mile down the tracks, assuming you don't follow us," he told the sergeant. "He'll be unharmed as long as we are."

"We'll find you," the sergeant shot back, eyes almost as smoldering as those of the cambions. "You killed two U.S. Army soldiers today. You'll get death for that."

Frank shrugged. "Already got that."

CHAPTER ELEVEN

The fountain in the front lawn of the White House had frozen solid, becoming a gleaming silver sculpture with a few drops of water plinking and plunking onto the ice at the bottom. The ornamental plants and finely cut grass had all turned brown, shriveling and wilting in the frigid January air. Behind it, the white house looked more gray than white, with frost glittering on its windows and the whole building taking on the color of long-dead bone.

A few people milled around on the lawn, but the D.C. Metro Police patrolled the grounds in their long coats of blue wool, twin columns of brass buttons shining in the sunlight.

"Stay back, please," they told everyone, Frank's group included. "Scarlet fever's in the White House. Can't have the whole city getting sick."

"You'd think security might be tighter," Spike muttered.

"They have no reason to suspect anything's wrong." Mills leaned against the fountain, his suit blending almost perfectly with the gray stone. "As far as they're concerned, the only danger is the fever."

Frank only half heard him, his mind drifting to the fight on the train. He'd killed an innocent man, a soldier doing his duty. A man who might have had a wife. Children.

"Frank?" Spike put his hand on Frank's shoulder. "You all right?"

Frank shook himself and nodded. Camille, Spike, Stan, Curtis, and Mills all stared at him. Camille chewed her lower lip, and Curtis looked like he might run and hug Frank again.

"Yeah, just thinking."

"You did what you had to do, Frank." Mills turned down the corners of his mouth. "Take it from someone on good terms with the Head Honcho, things like this aren't as black-and-white as you might think."

Frank spat on the frozen grass. "I should have found another way. He didn't need to die."

"Ain't your place to say that." Mills' eyes narrowed. "You were protecting Curtis. Let it go."

Motion in the corner of Frank's eye made him turn to see Corbett striding down the frosted street, boot heels clacking on the stones. His eyes glittered like black ice, and his grin seemed stretched a bit too far. He walked straight up to Spike and gave the big bartender a hug. Spike looked away, his smile awkward.

Mills stepped forward, hands on hips. "Where'd you run off to?" The look on the man's face made Frank's teeth ache.

"I did some digging around," he told them, eyes flitting over the group, counting heads. "Needed more information than old Mills here was picking up."

Mills shot him a withering glare. "And where did this investigating take you?"

Corbett's grin grew even wider. "When you need information, ask soldiers. They live or die based on what they know about their surroundings, and they can be coaxed into talking about it with just a little whiskey.

"I found a group of soldiers in a tavern not far from here. Soldiers who helped prepare for the President Hayes funeral security."

Mills shook his head, irritation creeping into his voice. "You aren't supposed to go off on your own."

Corbett frowned, but recovered quickly. "I know. But these soldiers worked security for this end of the procession, and they heard rumors of a threat to the president. Said something about conspirators meeting at one of the locations Booth and his people used during the assassination attempt."

"They told you this?" Mills asked, eyebrows raised.

"With a bit of convincing using our boss' power."

Mills threw up his hands. "We're not supposed to use His power on mortals like that, Sergeant! Do you never listen?"

This time, Corbett's smile melted like ice in the sun. "They didn't notice a thing, Mills. They'd already searched Ford's Theater, the Surratt boarding house, National Hotel, and Herndon House, but didn't find a thing."

Mills faced them. "That pretty much covers all of Booth's old stomping grounds but one."

Corbett grinned. "The Garrett Farm."

Frank raised an eyebrow at Mills, who rubbed his

temples. "When Booth jumped from the balcony to the stage, he broke his leg and needed care, so he stopped at a farm where he knew the owner. He was eventually cornered and killed there by our very own Sergeant Corbett."

"But I got that information yesterday," Corbett said. "Booth and his boys could be gone by now."

"Then, we'll have to split up." Frank looked at Mills. "You can't hurt a living human, but can you do anything to protect the president?"

Mills nodded. "There may be some ways we can help."

"Then, stay here and try your best to warn someone." Frank turned to Camille. "Take Curtis and check Ford's Theater and some of those other locations. See if the soldiers missed anything."

She frowned. "I get babysitting duty?"

Curtis huffed and crossed his arms, making Frank chuckle.

"Spike, Stan, and I will check out this Garrett Farm. We meet back here this evening."

* * *

The Garrett Farm stood atop an overgrown hill just outside of Port Royal. Frank and his group kneeled in the underbrush at the base of the hill, staring up at the white clapboard siding and vacant front porch, breath steaming the air before their faces.

"Booth died right there on that porch," Stan said.

Frank nodded. Chimneys at either end stood cold against the graying sky as the sun fell, and shadows stretched through the woods around them. Frank shivered, and not from the cold. He felt death here.

"Don't look like anyone's there," Spike muttered,

rubbing his hands together to warm them. "No light, front door's wide open. No movement."

Behind them, a twig snapped, making all three men wheel, guns raised. A shadow flitted from tree to tree.

"Who's there?" Stan spoke before Frank could shush him. His voice echoed through the empty woods, a bell tolling their presence to anyone—and anything—nearby.

Slowly, yellow eyes gleaming in the dusky light, Batcho limped toward them, favoring his front leg. He bled from a dozen wounds, but he growled as he approached, hackles raised, eyes locked on the Garrett house.

He brushed against Frank, and the gunfighter let his fingers run through the coyote's fur. They came away coated in blood.

"He's hurt," Stan noted. "Real bad."

"And yet, he's here." Spike stared at Batcho with something akin to awe in his eyes. "And he knows us."

"I thought you were dead," Frank said to the guide.

Batcho looked back over his shoulder and whined.

"We should go," Spike suggested. "Get Batcho some help. There's nothing here. Place is empty."

Batcho continued to stare at the house, and let out another low growl.

Frank shook his head. "He smells something. We'd better check it out."

Frank took the lead, Batcho at his side, while Spike and Stan followed. The steps to the sagging front porch creaked, making Frank wince with every footfall. The interior was already dark, dusty blades of orange evening sun slicing through the shadows where windows allowed it, forming circles of light on the floor.

The door opened into the sitting room, where plain, wooden chairs sat, covered in blankets of dust. Batcho growled again, gazing through the room, deeper into the home. The group crept through the small foyer, through an empty dining room, into a spacious kitchen, where an old, iron wood stove sat cold and silent against the back wall.

Two men's bodies sprawled on the floor, dressed in nothing more than their boxers, single bullet holes in their chests. A lake of half-frozen blood coated the tile, spread in a circle under the bodies.

Batcho growled again, and refused to enter the room. Gun raised, Frank stepped forward and kneeled by the closest body, feeling the neck for a pulse. He found none, only cold, hard flesh. Stan knelt beside the other corpse.

"This one's been dead awhile," Frank said, standing. "Cold and stiff."

Stan stayed on his knees, searching the third body with long fingers. He put his ear to the man's naked chest, checked his wrist, and even listened for breath. His eyes flashed blue as he did, telling Frank he was using his power.

"Is he alive?" Frank asked.

Stan shook his head. "No, but he passed recently. Body's still warm, and not stiff yet."

His eyes glowed a steady blue now, as his hands danced over the dead man's skin. "I might be able to bring him back just enough to peek into his mind. Maybe we can figure out who these men are and what happened to them."

Frank examined their faces, finding similar jawlines and noses. "They look like siblings. I assume we're looking at two of the Hammonds."

Stan nodded. "That doesn't tell us what happened, though. And since Booth's people probably abandoned these bodies, we might be able to tell whose bodies they control now."

"And that might tell us what they're up to." Frank holstered his pistol and cracked the knuckles on his gun hand.

The stage driver made a pained expression as he ran his fingers through the coagulating blood on the floor, then drew an upside down star on the dead man's chest. More blood, and another star on the forehead. He worked quickly, scribing letters Frank didn't recognize around the body, on the arms, legs, stomach, and face. When it was done, Stan looked up at Frank and Spike.

"Y'all might want to step back for this. Doesn't always go as planned."

Frank complied, using his arm to nudge Spike back, as well. Stan used his fingers to pry open the dead man's eyes. Frank was surprised for some reason to see a normal, average green color, rather than a midnight black or glowing red, but Stan's own eyes pulsed with blue light as he leaned over and stared deep into the corpse's eyes.

Stan muttered a chant under his breath, something in a language Frank didn't recognize.

After a few words, blue tears dripped from Stan's eyes into those of the corpse, lending them their ghostly glow.

"They took over the bodies of police officers," Stan announced, gaze still locked with the cadaver before him. "Washington Metro officers. Booth's men met them at a bar. I can see them talking, but there's no sound. I have to read lips.

"Something about their assignment tomorrow. On the twentieth."

Without warning, Stan's body stiffened and the light

in his eyes flared brighter, twin beams of blue linking his eyes to the dead man's. His face contorted in pain.

"Stan!" Frank rushed to his side, reaching for his shoulder, but not quite touching him.

"Trap," Stan managed through gritted teeth.

He strained against the body, arms pushing him back, but no matter how the muscles in his neck bulged, he couldn't look away. Slowly, inexorably, an inky mist crawled up the light columns from the dead man's eyes, making their way toward Stan's.

"How can we help?" Spike's voice shook as he rushed to kneel beside the stage driver. "Tell us what to do."

Stan shook his head. "Too late," he gasped. "They've got me. Run!"

A second Stan—an ethereal copy of him—began to detach itself from his body, swirling like a miniature tornado toward the dead man's eyes. Stan wailed in agony.

Frank's stomach lurched, but he drew his pistol. He waved Spike back, and fired a shot into the corpse's right eye. The column of light winked out, and Stan managed to turn his head ever so slightly. But it wasn't enough, and the shadow-Stan had almost detached itself from his body. Wincing, Frank shot out the man's second eye.

Stan flew back from the body, soaring across the room and crashing into the far wall. He slid to the floor and lay still.

Frank and Spike exchanged a worried glance, the bartender's huge hands tightening their grip on his shotgun, but neither man moved. A moment later, Stan groaned and sat up.

"I don't know how you thought of that, gunfighter, but I owe you."

Frank pulled the thin man to his feet.

"Who set the trap?"

Stan walked around the kitchen, stopping to squat against a wooden table, head bowed.

"Booth himself, I think. It was darn clever, too. Once you're inside the mind of a dead person, your vision is limited. You can only see so far ahead, and almost not at all to the sides. Easy to set a spell there, out of sight."

Fire burned in Frank's gut.

"Mr. Booth and me, we're gonna have a real palaver about this," he muttered. "Just before I put an ounce of lead in between his eyes."

Stan straightened and managed a weak smile. Batcho finally entered the room, crossed to the driver, and licked his face.

"Somethin' tells me that might not be Booth's only trap," Spike warned. "He's a smart one. He ain't likely to leave much to chance."

Frank agreed. "Let's find the others. Tomorrow's Sunday and we need to be at that church."

Stan picked up a matchbook off the table. He read it, and tossed it to Frank.

"National Hotel," Frank read. "Pennsylvania and Sixth in Washington."

"Not far from the White House," Stan explained. "Perfect spot for planning an assassination."

"I guess we know where we're going, then." Frank holstered his gun and strode from the room.

CHAPTER TWELVE

"Mills said he'd meet us here."

Camille's eyes narrowed as she peered down the alley, the slanting morning sun exaggerating shadows and making the alley a patchwork of dark and light. Frank admired her face—still pretty, despite being dead and wearing no makeup—until she caught him looking and frowned. "You oughta be watching for Mills. Or for Booth and his people."

Beside him, Frank noticed Curtis grinning at the two of them, freckles glinting in the sunlight.

Frank snickered and looked deep into the alley. They'd met up with Camille and Curtis as soon as they'd gotten back from the Garrett Farm, the blonde telling them Mills was in the White House and would meet them in the morning.

So, they'd left the coyote to heal in the hotel room and come here.

Above them, the National Hotel's wall rose four stories, a hulking mass of red brick and glass that blotted out all but a sliver of blue. Frost glittered where sun touched brick.

Movement caught his eye, far down the alley. Mills stepped from the shadows, arms bound behind him, a gag over his mouth. Mist the color of a thundercloud wrapped around him, swirling as if it had a life of its own.

Mills struggled against the bonds, and the mist contracted, like a boa constrictor crushing its prey.

Frank and his friends surged forward, but before they'd gone ten feet, a second figure appeared.

Dressed in an all-black soldier's uniform, three blood-red stripes on each sleeve, Boston Corbett hardly looked like the same wan, slender man Frank had seen before. His shoulders bunched with muscle now, his neck ropy and taut, as if he strained just holding his head up. His skin had turned the color of midnight, his lips a deathly gray, his eyes pools of blood. Sharp claws raked at the fabric of his own pants, and long fangs dug into his lower lip, making rivulets of blood run down his chin.

"That's no angel," Spike muttered, shotgun coming up. Stan raised his rifle, and Camille's Bowie snicked from its sheath.

"How right you are!" Corbett raised his arms over his head, pointing to the heavens, and tossed back his head. His hair had turned white as frost, cascading down his back like a river of ice. "It seems The Head Honcho disapproved of my behavior, and threatened to toss me down from Heaven.

"But I never did care much for all those rules and restrictions, so I did what no one expected: I jumped. Yep, I suppose I'm not really a 'fallen angel' if I did the falling of my own accord."

Frank drew his pistol, but wasn't sure it would do any good. With his left hand, he eased Curtis behind him. Camille, Spike, and Stan all stepped forward until the boy was completely hidden.

"So, what are you, then? And what's your beef with us?"

Corbett scrunched his brow a bit, scratching his chin with one claw.

"You know, I'm not rightly sure what I am, at least right now. Booth said his boss would give me certain powers so long as I promised to stop you and your friends from stopping him.

"And I suppose that answers your second question."

"Your boss?" Frank took a step back. "Who might that be?"

Corbett laughed. "By the time you find out, it'll be too late!"

Green lightning jumped from his fingertips to the ground, making the hair on Frank's neck stand up. If the color meant what it did for Frank's bullets, the gunfighter knew what would happen to anyone it touched.

He turned to Stan. "Get Curtis and yourself out of here. Something tells me this ain't gonna end well, and you still have lives to live."

Curtis opened his mouth to protest, but Frank shushed him with a wave of his hand and turned back to Corbett. Still, neither the driver nor the boy moved.

"I thought you wanted Booth sent back, too?"

Corbett's grin exposed more of his blood-soaked

fangs. "I never recovered from the punishment they tried to heap on me for killin' Booth. They ostracized me, Butcher. Made me an outsider. That wears on a man. Even the Head Honcho had his doubts about me or I'd be an angel by now."

Corbett lifted his hands over his head and lightning arced from his fingertips to the sky, blasting chips of brick from the hotel side, and showering them down on Frank and his posse. Frank shielded Curtis with his body until the chips were done flying.

"I told you two to get out of here," he whispered as he rose to face Corbett. "Do it!"

Curtis turned to run back the way they'd come, but Frank heard him skid to a stop.

Stan pointed in the direction Curtis had run. "You'd better look at this, Frank."

Frank turned, keeping his pistol pointed at the fallen angel. Blocking the end of the alley stood a dozen or so soldiers, all in blue uniforms with long, navy blue coats, twin rows of brass buttons shining in the morning sun. Each held a carbine in his hands, aimed at Frank's group.

When Frank turned back to Corbett, another six soldiers stood in front of the one-time sergeant. All wore blank expressions.

"I could control even more," Corbett said, "but these are enough to destroy you and your friends."

"We're already dead, Corbett." Frank spit the words at his feet. "What more could your little puppet soldiers do to us?"

Corbett chuckled and looked at Spike. "Most of them? Nothing. They're distractions for the ones using those special green bullets I got from his pocket."

Frank winced. Of course, the hug. It had seemed so out of place at the time. Now, it made perfect sense—

he'd stolen the extra bullets Buzzy had given Spike.

Frank studied the soldiers. Most were young, barely more than boys, with baby-fat cheeks and jawlines free of stubble. The thought of shooting them, of killing more innocents guilty only of being under someone else's control, made him shiver. And the thought of Curtis being caught in the crossfire was even worse.

"Just let us go, Sergeant. We'll be on our way and let Booth do his business. No skin off my nose."

"Frank! We can take these guys." Curtis' voice seemed small, lost in the tense silence of the alley. "What are you doing?"

"Saving your hide, kid."

Quick as a flash, Curtis grabbed Frank's hand and pulled the trigger.

The gun kicked, hitting Frank between the eyes, and dazing him. He managed to tackle the boy to the ground just as the shooting started.

One round dug its way into Frank's ribs, just under his right armpit, but since he didn't disappear in a vortex of green light, Frank assumed it was just normal lead. Shoving Curtis between stacks of garbage, Frank rolled to his knees and fired off three rounds at Corbett.

Even as Frank fanned the hammer on his Colt, a soldier jumped in front of Corbett, absorbing all three shots dead center in his chest. As he died, his soul was ripped from his body with a terrifying shriek, swirling up into the clear slice of blue sky above them where it dissipated like fog. The body fell limp to the street.

Frank fired again and again, moving as he did so, sending a storm of lead at the fallen angel in the span of a few heartbeats, but Corbett was quicker, and soldiers appeared in front of him for every round, souls torn from their bodies with horrible screams and fading from existence.

In a few seconds, a pile of bodies lay at Corbett's feet, all felled by Frank's bullets. With a thought, Frank changed to regular bullets. Maybe he could wound the men enough to keep them out of the fight, but not enough to kill them. And especially not enough to wipe souls from existence. Then, he could go after Corbett.

He shot again, hitting one man in the thigh, but if he noticed, the soldier didn't show it. He stood tall and fired back. This time, Frank rolled to his right, gun coming up in a hurry. He plugged the soldier in the chest, and another immediately took his place.

Behind him, Frank heard rifles firing and out the corner of his eye, he noted Camille standing in front of Curtis, who still hid between trash piles. A moment later, no soldiers remained standing. Spike bled from wounds in his shoulder and thigh, while blood ran down Stan's forehead.

Between Corbett and the others, Mills had dropped to his knees, struggling against his bonds. He looked Frank in the eye for an instant before toppling onto his back.

"See, gunfighter?" Corbett's laugh was almost a growl. "You're right back to killing, right back to your nature. It's all you know. Hell, you're gonna get your friends here killed, too, you're so good at this."

"At least I'll kill you, too."

Corbett laughed again, this time louder, like a series of thunderclaps echoing down the alley. He snapped his fingers and suddenly, Curtis was there, in his arms. Corbett held the barrel of a pistol to the boy's head and sneered. A line of soldiers ran from the alley behind him, forming a half-circle in front of the fallen angel.

"And what about this one?" He pushed the barrel

tighter against Curtis' head. "You'll have to kill all these soldiers and the boy to get to me. But isn't that what Hell's Butcher does?"

Frank's gun had lowered, his arm now limp at his side. His shoulders slumped, and his eyes traced patterns on the cobblestones.

"You three walk away from this now," Corbett shouted, "and I'll let the boy live. Hell, I might even help him find a nice home to stay in. All you have to do is go back to Hell, where you belong, and leave Booth to his business."

On the ground between them, Mills sat up, locking eyes with Frank. He winked. Or at least, Frank thought he did.

But he couldn't risk Curtis' life.

"We'll do it. Let Stan take Curtis, release those soldiers, and us three will pull the trigger on ourselves. You have my word."

Corbett threw back his head and laughed at the heavens. "The word of a gunfighter? You can't be serious! No, Frank, I think—"

Curtis dug his teeth into the fallen angel's arm. Corbett cried out and the boy slipped from his grasp, dashing past the soldiers in a heartbeat.

Frank and his group opened fire, their first few shots ripping into Corbett with flashes of green before the soldiers ringed him in, several falling before Frank waved for his friends to cease fire.

Corbett's face twisted with rage, lightning bolts jumping from his fingertips.

"You'll pay for that, gunfighter! Where's that boy?"

Frank searched the alley, but Curtis had disappeared.

"Guess you'll have to settle for destroying us." Frank

raised his pistol again. "Come out from your flesh fort and fight, coward."

Corbett's reply came in the form of a lightning bolt loosed at the gunfighter. Frank managed to dive out of the way, but the crackling heat singed his eyebrows and turned the frigid air hot and dry.

Frank rolled to his feet, firing again, but soldiers moved into the bullets' paths and two fell dead. Frank winced, but kept firing, killing more soldiers as they jumped to fill gaps in the wall around Corbett.

Corbett's next bolt struck at Spike's feet and hurled him back, out of the alley. The big man landed with a *whump* as Frank fired again. This time, though, no soldier got in the way, and Frank's bullet struck Corbett on the cheek.

The fallen angel's head snapped left, then back at Frank, his eyes draining of their color until they were a white as pure as the snow.

"That can't be good," Stan muttered, aiming the Sharps rifle at their target.

"Wait for the lightning," Frank muttered. "He can't keep the soldiers under control when he throws it."

Corbett's hands swept up, fingers spread wide, and streaks of green fire jumped toward Frank's group. They all fired at once, the rounds tearing into Corbett's chest, shoulder, and leg.

But they paid the price, the lightning hammering down around them. Camille cried out as smoke rose from her charred shoulder. Stan was knocked against the wall and fell, unconscious. Frank managed to stay upright, but almost wished he hadn't.

Corbett's face twisted with rage, and he flexed every muscle in his body, as if straining against bonds, until five lead bullets emerged from his body and landed with plinks in the street. The corners of his mouth turned up and his blank stare settled on Frank.

"You're out of allies, Marshal. And out of time."

Lightning sparked from his hands, log-thick columns of electricity this time, arcing through the air, bound straight for their target. Time slowed down, and Frank's motion became drawn out, slowed like he was standing in a vat of syrup. He watched the crackling bolts inch closer, and knew he couldn't possibly get out of the way in time. Corbett was about to wipe his soul from existence.

Then, Mills appeared, diving in front of Frank. Time snapped back to normal as the angel raised his hands to catch the lightning bolts. He shuddered under their impact, dropping to one knee, fighting with every ounce of strength he had. But he held, drawing the lightning into himself. It sparked and sizzled around him, and he cried out in agony as it burned him. Corbett pumped more and more into his one-time partner, but Mills took it all, wrapped it around him like a blanket, and screamed.

Corbett stopped, hands on his hips, and watched as Mills struggled with the power around him. He shook his head.

"You're an angel, Mills. You can't touch this kind of power and survive it. It'll destroy you."

Mills rose to his feet, his spine straight, arms outstretched. Lightning whizzed around him now, faster and faster, until it made a humming noise like nothing Frank had ever heard.

The angel looked back over his shoulder.

"Shoot for the heart, Frank," he managed between clenched teeth. "You'll only get one shot."

Frank nodded and cocked the hammer on his Colt.

With a cry, Mills hurled the blanket of power away from him in a pillar of green. It hammered into Corbett's line of soldiers, scorching a hole and striking the fallen angel in the chest.

"Now!" Mills collapsed as he yelled.

Frank fired one shot. As the bullet tore into Corbett's chest, his eyes opened wide and he gaped. Emerald light swirled around him now, out of control, and Corbett fought it, thrashing and crying out as the green tried to destroy his soul.

He tossed his head back and tore at the green light, ripping it from his body in tatters. Finally, he took off down the alley, disappearing into the shadows.

Frank rushed to Mills, kneeling, and cradling his head in his lap. The detective looked up at him and smiled.

Mills laughed, a sound that turned to a cough instantly.

"Who'd have thought, Heaven and Hell working together?"

Frank nodded. "Damned strange. Not sure either of our bosses would like it."

Mills shrugged. "Mine's right cross at me for killing those soldiers."

Frank cleared his throat and looked away. "Can't imagine he'd care much for me at all then."

"Go easy on yourself." He coughed and his eyes fluttered like me might pass out, but he winced, swallowed hard, and went on. "You ain't no butcher, no matter what that fool said. Now listen.

"Booth's been meeting with all the old rebel sympathizers he met with for the assassination. Well, those that are still alive. He has an army of rebels scattered all around the city, ready to rise up when he kills the president."

"Did you find out where?"

Mills shook his head. "But it'll be tomorrow. Sunday. You gotta stop him, Frank. This is bigger than just an escaped soul starting trouble. It runs deep through that place you call home now. Trouble's brewing down there."

"What kind of trouble?"

Mills coughed again, the hacks wracking his body, making him convulse and double over.

He pressed his revolver into Frank's palm.

"Shoots straight every time."

"Mills, what kind of trouble?"

But the detective's head fell back into Frank's lap, his face turning an ashen gray. Frank eased him to the ground, and stood. As soon as he did, Mills' body turned to snow and blew away, down the alley.

Camille and Stan watched, a few feet away. Behind them, a dazed but alive Spike wandered back into the alley.

"You beat 'im," Spike said.

"Mills beat him," Frank corrected. "I just helped."

"Where's Curtis?" Camille searched the alley, eyes wide.

Frank shrugged. "He's at home on the streets. He'll find his way to us."

"What now?" Spike looked like he'd been run over by a horse, with a flap of skin hanging dead from his forehead.

Frank took a deep breath, then patted the Colt at his hip.

"Now, we find some answers, damn it."

CHAPTER THIRTEEN

Frank kicked in the door to the tavern and stormed inside, pistol drawn, bandana over his face. Behind him, Camille, Spike, and Stan burst in, rifles cocked and ready.

The few patrons of the tiny hole-in-the-wall place stopped what they were doing and stared, some with mugs or glasses halfway to their lips. A fiddler in the back played a scraggly-sounding note, then let the music die. Most of the ten or so men were soldiers, dressed in full-length blue wool jackets. Silence wrapped the place like a death shroud.

The bartender's hand drifted toward the underside of the bar, but Spike took aim at his head with his shotgun.

"Wouldn't be wise, mister."

The bartender raised his hands and backed away.

"We ain't here to rob you," Frank shouted. "We just need some information. Some of you might have talked to a man the other night—tall fella, dark hair, eyes like a graveyard. He asked you about the president. We need to ask those men some questions."

At first, no one moved, so Frank cleared his throat.

"The sooner someone talks to us, the sooner we're out of your hair, and no one gets hurt."

Two soldiers at a table near the fiddler stood, one of them clearing his throat.

"We talked to him."

"Come with us," Frank ordered.

Outside, the men shivered and blew in their hands, stamping their feet for warmth. They eyed Frank and his friends suspiciously, their soldier instincts keen to things that weren't quite right. Their hands hovered near the revolvers on their hips.

Frank ushered the men to a streetlamp, hoping the light would give them some comfort, and leaned in close.

"I'm Corporal Palmer." The larger one—an imposing man with dirty blond hair and eyes the color of chipped jade—took the lead. "What do you need?"

The other was a smaller man, with greasy black hair and eyes almost as dark.

"We think there will be an attempt on President Harrison's life tomorrow," Frank said. Both men straightened, their interest piqued. "Our informant says it'll happen away from the White House, so we need to know where the president might go on a Sunday."

The men exchanged a glance, and Palmer looked Frank in the eye.

"How do we know you aren't the ones gonna kill

him?"

"I'm Marshal Frank Butcher, and my job is to stop the killers."

"Wouldn't be the first crooked marshal we'd seen around here."

Frank took a deep breath and fought down his temper. He was short on time, but losing his patience with this man wouldn't help things. Palmer was just doing his job.

He put his hand on the corporal's shoulder and looked him in the eye. "Look, the man you talked to turned on us. He's working with conspirators and southern sympathizers here in the city. They're hoping to kill President Harrison and start themselves a new rebellion."

Again, Palmer and his partner looked at one another, but this time, Frank caught something pass between them, some sort of cautionary silence. The air thrummed with tension for a heartbeat, then both soldiers bolted.

Spike reacted first, sticking his meaty arm out so the smaller soldier clotheslined himself and fell to the street, motionless. Palmer, though, streaked away. Frank knew he couldn't catch him—he wasn't fleet of foot when he was alive, and now, with his dead body stiff in the cold, he had no chance.

Stan's eyes caught fire, blue light spilling onto the street, making Frank squint at the sudden brightness. The stage driver thrust his arm forward, fingers spread, then made a fist.

Down the street, Palmer jerked to a stop as if someone had grabbed his collar. Stan flexed his arm like he was pulling something toward him, and at the same time, Palmer started sliding backward. His boot heels dragged on the street, his arms flailing at his sides. He reached for his sidearm, but a flick of Stan's other hand sent the pistol clattering across the street.

With a final jerk of his arm, Stand spun the soldier to face Frank. Palmer's eyes were wide as platters and his lips moved in silence.

"The Lord is my shepherd, I shall not w-w-want."

Frank leaned in so his face was just an inch from the frightened soldier's. He slid down his kerchief so the man could see the rotted skin around his mouth, and the decayed teeth inside.

"Now listen here, Corporal. Seems to me you're part of this rebellion. No other reason for you to run than that. So, I could turn you over to my friend, or you could tell me what I need to know."

Palmer hesitated, eyes searching for answers. This time when he prayed, a southern lilt tinged his words.

"He maketh me to lie down in green pastures."

Frank sighed. "Or my friends and I could keep you for ourselves. I could let Stan here, the one whose power is holding you, work some of his magic on you. Let's see if your God's rod and staff are comforting then."

Palmer's teeth started to chatter and he jerked his head from side to side, trying to find Stan in his peripheral vision.

"First Presbyterian!" He blurted, spit flying from his lips. "They're gonna kill him at church, when he's there praying for his daughter to heal."

Frank looked deep into Palmer's eyes, detected only fear, no deceit. So, he smiled.

"Stan?"

"Yeah, Marshal?"

"See to it our friends here don't remember any of this come mornin'."

Stan grinned.

CHAPTER FOURTEEN

Frank peered around the lamppost through the falling snow at the hulking, monolithic structure of the First Presbyterian Church, also known as the National Presbyterian Church, and shook his head. Made of cold, gray granite, the building looked as much like a fortress as it did a chapel. Wide stairs led up to arched doorways, with thick, cherry wood doors closed against the winter cold. The bell tower on the left had a smaller arched door, with tiny windows that would allow a sniper to shoot at the street from relative safety.

Sunlight glinted off the stained glass windows and icicles that hung from the eaves, and as Frank listened, the church bells tolled, announcing it was time for nine o-clock services. On cue, as soon as the bells stopped, a choir's muffled voice came from inside the formidable church.

"What do we do?" Stan stamped his feet beside them, clapping his gloved hands together for warmth. "There are enough policemen out there to stop the Army."

Frank had to agree. At least fifty armed Metro Police stood near the front of the church, rifles at the ready. They paced around the steps and the plaza in front of the church, eyes always moving.

"Yeah, looks like someone got word of the plot." Frank spat. He knew if he'd been alive, he'd likely be shivering like Stan. As it was, his body was stiff and lumbering, both from lack of sleep and the cold. "Maybe the president's safe in there, after all."

"You know that ain't true." Camille glanced at him sidelong. "Man like Booth don't give up so easy."

Beside her, Spike grunted assent.

"Any sign of Curtis yet?" The barkeep frowned, wrinkling the corners of his eye.

Camille shook her head, brow furrowed.

A group of people stepped out of a side street and onto Connecticut Avenue, striding right for them. They walked with a purpose, a tall man in his Sunday finest leading two uniformed policemen. Frank counted three men and one child being dragged between them. He kicked and fussed, glaring like a roped cat, but the men who held his arms paid him no heed.

Camille gasped and Spike straightened.

"Curtis," Frank muttered. "What have you gotten yourself into?"

Booth's gang, one John Hammond and two Metro Policemen, turned right and stopped at the base of the church steps. Another police officer approached, but John Hammond raised an arm and the man stopped in his tracks. The possessed policemen raised their arms too, palms out in front of them, and the other cops around the church snapped to attention.

"They know we're here," Spike muttered.

The gang flicked their wrists and as one, all fifty police officers turned and faced Frank's group.

"Yep." Frank drew his Colt. "Spread out and—"

As he spoke, three figures dropped from the roof of the Church, sliding down the slate shingles, spreading leathery wings, and sinking to the street on either side of the gang. The cambions glared at Frank, eyes locked on him with fires of rage burning inside. They were all males this time, including the one Frank had wounded, licking his lips and taut with bloodlust. The other two he hadn't seen before, but they looked like they knew him.

"They look mighty angry," Stan took aim at one with his Sharps. Frank eased his rifle down.

"That ain't gonna stop 'em. Save your ammo for the policemen. Shoot to wound, if you can. They're good men who can't stop themselves."

The Booth conspirators turned and strode up the steps as fifty carbine rifles rose and took aim at Frank's posse. As the group pushed through the church doors, Curtis shooting a pleading look over his shoulder, the officers opened fire.

Frank and his group scattered. Frank rolled to his right and came up firing, hitting one policeman in the knee, and a second in the shoulder. Each shot made his teeth gnash, and he took more time than he normally would. He aimed for non-lethal targets as lead ripped through the air around him. He missed more than he hit, but he kept shooting, throwing his own volley of lead at the attackers.

Stan had taken cover behind a planter, firing into the

crowd, dropping two men, while Spike fired the Winchester from behind an abandoned buggy. Camille was nowhere to be seen.

"We gotta get inside that chapel!" Frank yelled. "Curtis is in there!"

If the others heard him, they didn't acknowledge. He dropped one sergeant with a slug to the arm, and missed another. Behind the police, the cambions stood, glaring at him, towers of taut muscle and ropy sinew.

A bullet slammed into Frank's left shoulder, rocking him back. He nearly fell, but steadied himself and dropped the man with a slug to the thigh. Another round tore through his chest, exploding out his back, making Frank fall to one knee.

He was losing this way, by metering his shots and trying not to kill anyone. And if he lost, it meant Curtis died.

Growling, Frank levered himself to his feet and ripped off three shots at the nearest policeman. As soon as that one fell, Frank dropped two more, shooting for hearts and heads now. Tears streamed down his cheeks as he killed innocent men, fulfilling his own destiny — butchering them as he was meant to do. His enemies fell so fast, he actually heard the reduction in their gunfire. Spike and Stan advanced, coming out from their hiding spots, and marching steadily forward. Only a handful of police stood now, not nearly enough to stop the posse.

Seeing their guards down, the cambions took to flight and joined the fray.

If the possessed policemen had been mindlessly methodical, the halflings were the opposite: wild and random and vicious. Again, they moved so fast that Frank and his friends couldn't shoot them, only this time, they didn't grapple with their prey. Instead, they darted in quick and feral, slashing and biting before slipping back, out of reach. All in the blink of an eye, too.

Pain seared through Frank's flesh as the wounded one raked razor-sharp claws across his arms, shoulders, and back, always darting in just out of his view, then lurching back before Frank could retaliate. The claws shredded Frank's long coat and the clothing underneath became soaked and sticky with blood.

He saw Camille go down to her knees, a cambion beating her about the head and shoulders, while Spike and Stan did their best to fend off the last one, swinging at it with their rifles, ammo exhausted.

The cambion hit Frank on the left, the back, left again, then right, drawing blood each time, and further tightening Frank's already stiff muscles. Left, back, left, right.

Realization hit Frank like a locomotive: the attacks weren't random at all.

It struck from the left, pounded him in the back, went left again. But this time, Frank raised his pistol to the right and fired just as the half-demon appeared.

The cambion shrieked so loud, its partners stopped and looked at it, eyes wide, fangs dripping. Frank's bullet had ripped through its shoulder, and black blood ran down the surface of its skin like oil.

The cambion's eyes flashed brightly, and rage lit its already twisted face. It spread its wings and lifted off, hovering a few feet above him. Frank raised his pistol to shoot, but the cambion dove like a hawk, smashing him to the street. The wind rushed from his lungs. His pistol slid out of reach, and he barely caught the thing's wrists as it flailed at him, trying to gouge out his eyes.

It weighed as much as three men, and its rippling muscles were an easy match for Frank's long-dead body.

Slowly, deliberately, it pressed its claws inward, forcing Frank's arms together, until the sharp tips of its claws dug into his temples.

Beside him, Camille screamed and Spike roared like a caged beast. But Frank knew he was beat. He was no match for this creature of Hell. He lacked the strength, his weapon was gone, and his wounds cried out in agony.

As a warm trickle of blood rolled down his temple, Frank closed his eyes and prepared for the inevitable.

Another shriek ripped through the cold morning air, echoing off the church and making the cambion glance away. Then, something barreled into it, driving the beast off Frank's chest and onto the stones.

Frank rolled right, scooped up his gun, and came to his feet.

Squatting on the chest of the male cambion was the female, the one Frank had let go. Blood red cat-eyes glared down at the male, filled with malice and hate. She shrieked in the male's face and promptly tore out his throat with a clawed hand.

Then, she looked Frank in the eye and, for an instant, the red faded and her eyes became human again. Soft and brown, they bore into Frank for a heartbeat, then the red filled them again and she leapt away.

The female dispatched with the beast attacking Camille, while Frank rushed to Spike's aid. The cambion was so engrossed in its battle with Spike that it never saw Frank coming. It sat on the bartender's chest, clawed feet drawing blood from his ribs, while Spike fought to keep its hands from his neck.

Frank made sure his Colt held the glowing, green rounds, then cocked the hammer, put it to the back of the creature's head, and fired. The monster wailed, toppled off the bartender, and writhed in the street, green mist fighting it, trying to engulf it. Fear showed in the cambion's eyes an instant before the mist turned him to dust.

Frank helped Spike sit up. The big man bled from a dozen wounds, and a flap of skin had peeled from his forehead, flopping over one eye. Still, he brushed Frank's hands away.

"Help Camille!"

The female cambion had attached herself to the last male's back, and was gouging at his eyes, while Camille slashed at it with her Bowie. Frank almost pitied the monster, stuck between those two women.

"She has it under control." He pressed a kerchief to Spike's head, easing the skin flap back into place.

A moment later, Camille's Bowie found the cambion's heart and black blood gushed forth. Camille dodged it, and it hit the street, sizzling like bacon fat. The male cambion tried to roar as the green light from her knife consumed him, but the female jumped off just as he, too, turned to dust.

Frank rose and faced their new-found ally. The cambion crouched, ready to pounce, snarling and raking her blood-caked claws at the cobblestones. Frank holstered his pistol and dropped his hands to his side.

"Thanks."

If he was expecting more humanity from the demon-spawn, he didn't get it. She simply shrieked and drove herself skyward, flapping her tattered wings as she disappeared behind the buildings.

Frank used a second kerchief to bandage Spike's wound closed, then gathered his posse around him. The sound of hymns rose from the church, the parishioners singing to Heaven, gleefully ignorant how close Hell actually stood.

"We need to get in there," Frank said. "But there are probably more guards inside, and they'll be watching for us. We may have to fight our way to the president."

He cringed at the thought of shooting more innocent people.

"You gonna be all right doing this, Frank?" A rivulet of blood ran down Spike's forehead and into his eye where the big man wiped it off with the back of his gloved hand.

"Reckon I'll have to be. We need to send these souls back to Hell before they manage to re-start the war."

Spike and Stan reloaded. Frank picked up a fallen rifle and offered it to Camille, but the blonde shook her head and wiped blood from her knife on her trousers.

"I'll be just fine."

Frank had no doubt.

"What about Curtis?" Stan asked.

"He's your job," Frank said. "Use your powers and whatever else you need, but get that boy to safety as soon as possible. Don't come back for us, either. Just get him clear of the fighting."

Stan nodded, but still looked concerned. "My powers won't work inside the Head Honcho's house. And some of your gadgets might not work too well, either. At least, they won't be as powerful as they are outside. Head Honcho's strong in there."

Frank hadn't thought about that. If his gun didn't work in the church, how would he stop Booth?

He shook his head. He'd have to worry about that if it happened.

"We all go in different doors. I'll take the front. Camille and Stan on the right, Spike left. Whoever has the best shot at Booth or any of his compadres takes it."

"I'll go in the back." Camille flipped her Bowie in the air and caught it by the handle. "Every church has a back door that leads into the chapel from behind. Maybe I can sneak up on him."

Frank was about to protest her going without a gun when the singing inside turned to shouts. A shot rang out, and the screams got louder.

CHAPTER FIFTEEN

Frank sprinted for the front door as fast as his cold-stiffened legs would carry him. The others took off in different directions.

He bounded up the steps and threw his shoulder into the thick, frozen wood of the door. The door threw him back, rocking only a bit with the force of his blow. He jerked at the handles, but the doors were locked tight.

Inside, he heard a man's voice, polished and smooth, rise above the screams.

"Dearly beloved, we are gathered here today to bear witness to the destruction of one who goes against his own people, to gaze in wonder as a usurper of the natural order is ripped from his throne and torn asunder."

Frank dealt a kick to the center of the door. It creaked and heaved, but held fast.

"The man you see before you has sold us out!" The voice had to be Booth, or rather, Booth through the body he had claimed. "He would lift up the black man, the negro made to serve us in the fields and in our homes, and make him equal to us! He wants them to vote, to have say in who rules over us. This cannot be allowed. Can I get an Amen?"

The congregation answered in monotone unison, "Amen!"

Frank had heard enough. Making sure he had regular lead in his pistol, he aimed it at the lock and fanned the hammer as fast as he could. A few seconds later, a series of holes circled the brass lock.

This time, Frank's kick shattered the wood and the door flew open.

The congregation stood in their suits and Sunday dresses, staring ahead at a figure on the platform at the head of the chapel. Beside the altar stood the possessed John Hammond, his wavy, black hair only a hand-span higher than the podium itself. A thick moustache hung down on either side of his mouth, and dark eyes swept across the gathered audience, settling on Frank. In that moment, Frank knew Hammond was gone, for only the icy cold hate of a denizen of Hell could send such a shiver down Frank's spine as ran down it just then.

Arrayed on either side of him were the two Metro policemen, but it was what stood behind them that made Frank's throat constrict.

Two tall crosses rose above the stage, made of cherry wood, and gleaming where sun sliced through the stained glass and shone on the wood.

Hanging from the cross on the right was a man

Frank assumed was President Benjamin Harrison. His suit was rumpled, his white hair tussled and messy. His beard and moustache covered the entire bottom half of his face, and while the bags under his eyes spoke of fatigue, the eyes themselves bored holes in the back of John Wilkes Booth and the body he possessed.

Hanging on the left cross, tears streaming down his face, was Curtis.

"Ah, Marshal Butcher." Booth didn't look the least bit surprised to see Frank. In fact, he flashed a dashing smile. "Welcome. You're just in time."

With a thought, Frank switched to the green bullets, hoping to get a clear shot at the assassin. But Booth beat him to it.

With a snap of his fingers, the entire congregation — every man, woman, and child — turned and faced Frank. Most held rifles or pistols, and with an upward sweep of his hand, Booth made them all aim at Frank.

"You know you're a killer, don't you? That's why I kept children in the room. So that when they die, it's your fault. Your failure. Just like it was with…what was his name? Your boy?"

The word caught in Frank's throat. He couldn't speak the name of his own son.

Booth slipped a Derringer from his pocket and stood next to the president. Frank shook off his own malaise, his finger twitching on the trigger of his Colt.

One of the Metro policemen under Booth's control stood beside Curtis, his hand on the handle of a revolver at his side.

"I know how good you are, Butcher." Booth's grin grew as his confidence did, spreading his thick moustache across his face like light spreads across the plains at dusk. "I know that if I move my gun, you're fast enough to shoot me before I can kill President Harrison. But my compatriot here will shoot the boy at the same time. You'll have to choose, Frank. Which one to save, the president or the boy?"

His Derringer rose an inch.

"Oh, and if you're waiting for help from your posse..."

As he let the sentence trail off, one of possessed policemen reached behind the curtain and hauled Camille, Spike, and Stan out to the stage. All were bound and gagged, their guns gone. The sheath for Camille's Bowie hung empty on her hip.

"Now, that six-shooter of yours won't work in here like it would outside." Booth rambled now, confidence shifting to arrogance. "Those green bullets might kill Mr. Hammond's body, but I'll be able to slip right into someone else's body in no time flat. In fact, you'll have to kill everyone in here, and even then, I guarantee I'll possess that boy's body next. Then, I'll watch as you have to gun down another child."

Frank tried to stop his hands from trembling, but even his gun hand tremored, twitching and shaking the barrel of his Colt. Booth had him cornered. There was no way to save Curtis and the president.

He fell to his knees and looked at the cold, marble floor before him.

"If you let the boy and my friends go, we'll walk out. You can do what you want."

Booth straightened, shook his head. Frank's left hand brushed his pocket, finding the cold bulge of Mills' British revolver. The detective's words echoed in his mind.

It shoots true as cupid's arrows.

"You're not in a position to make demands, Mr.

Butcher. I'll kill who I want, when I want."

Even with the revolver, it was a longshot. Frank never could shoot with his left hand, and now, with that arm injured, he didn't know if he could even lift it to his shoulder.

"In fact, I think I'll kill the president, inhabit the tiny body of your young friend there, and make him kill himself while you watch."

Frank cringed at the thought of Curtis putting the Derringer to his temple. Even if he made the shot and took down the cop, Booth would be inside Curtis' body. Frank had no way of stopping him.

"Do you suppose suicide is still a sin if you're possessed when you do it?" Booth rambled on. He was enjoying this now, savoring the scent of Frank's fear, the taste of his defeat. "For all we know, young Curtis here could be joining you in Hell when this is all done."

The cross. Curtis remained suspended from the cross. A symbol of God. The Head Honcho's own sigil, where he'd surrendered his only son.

Would he allow another to die that way?

Frank slipped his left hand into his pocket, wrapped his fingers around the cold steel of the revolver. He'd have to hope not.

"Well, Butcher. What do you have to say for yourself?"

Frank raised his head and looked Booth in the eye.

"I reckon I'll be takin' you in."

He drew lightning-fast, his Colt ripping off a round faster than a blink, the British revolver firing a second later. Lead ripped into John Hammond's forehead, exploding out the back of his head, spattering a startled President Harrison as it did.

The cop managed to raise his pistol about halfway

before the .38 caliber round struck his temple. He fell like a sack of potatoes.

The congregation members blinked and looked around, Booth's hold on them broken. Dazed, they muttered questions and shrugged. Some prayed, others wept.

Then, a cloud of midnight rose from Hammond's body as Booth's spirit raced toward the ceiling. It dashed through the rafters and streaked about as if lost, its motions speaking of anger, rage.

Frank took out the lasso and moved toward Curtis. He still wasn't a cowboy, and knew he stood as much chance of missing as anything, but he had to try.

Booth's soul saw Curtis, wailed in agony, and shot toward the boy.

Frank's legs pumped as he neared Curtis, but he was too late. The inky cloud smashed into the boy's body, rocking the cross on its mount. It wavered side to side, but did not fall.

Booth's soul stopped cold at Curtis' body, unable to go farther. It struggled and writhed, trying to force its way into Curtis, but the cross protected it.

Pocketing the revolver, Frank tossed the lasso, aiming for the cloud itself, but the rope missed left, and Booth's soul streaked for a window.

Frank followed, six-shooter in one hand, lariat in the other. He threw again, as the soul slipped through the glass, but the rope bounced off the pane harmlessly.

He fired, shattering the glass, and leapt through behind Booth's soul. Frank skidded to a stop in the snow-covered street. His jaw dropped and his gun hand fell an inch.

Facing him stood a squad of Metro police, probably twenty of them, their navy blue coats stark against the snow, brass buttons gleaming in the dim morning light. They wheeled, confusion painting their faces, as the gang poured out the side door.

Booth wasted no time, slipping into the nearest policeman like his skin was made of cheesecloth. The man straightened, his body rigid for an instant, then relaxed and turned slowly to face Frank. His eyes went from winter blue to deathly black, and a sadistic grin bent up the corners of his lips.

"Clever move, Butcher." Frank didn't know what the officer's voice might have sounded like normally, but this was all Booth, clear and dripping with showmanship. "You knew the cross would protect the boy. But it won't protect anyone out here."

Stan, Spike, and Camille stumbled out of the church and lined up on either side of Frank. Spike and Stan held their rifles, while Camille flipped the Bowie around on her fingers, its green-glowing blade a blur.

Spike pumped his shotgun. "We're a might outnumbered."

"I don't want to kill them all," Frank said. "Wound them only, if possible."

"And that's your weakness, Marshal." Booth's voice held a performer's edge, projected for everyone in the street to hear. And there was quite an audience, with parishioners and passersby all stopping to look. "You care about mortal lives, and it will be your undoing. I, however, do not."

He raised his hands to the sides and each officer took aim with a rifle or pistol at Frank and his group.

"I'm going back inside to kill the president," Booth snarled, moving back toward the chapel. "And your friend, too. My friends here will keep you company."

Frank scanned the gathered policemen and knew it

was hopeless. Their blank stares told him wounding them wouldn't be enough. They'd have to kill each one to get them to stop, and that was something Frank couldn't accept.

He had one chance. Chambering a green round with a thought, Frank pulled back the hammer on his pistol.

"You made one mistake, Booth." Frank smiled as Booth slowed.

"What's that, Marshal?"

"You left the church. Out here, my gun works just fine."

With a single motion, he brought up the gun and fired. Booth darted toward the church, but Frank had anticipated that and led him with the shot.

The bullet slammed into the policeman's chest, throwing him backward. As he landed on the stone street, green fire wrapped around his body like a hundred hissing snakes, writhing and twisting around limbs and torso and even his head.

Booth screamed, and the policeman's flesh sizzled. The smell of burning skin and hair made Frank wrinkle his nose. Something was wrong—it hadn't gone this way with the prospector, when he'd destroyed his soul. It was almost like the officer was suffering.

The man crawled on his belly toward Frank, fingernails digging into the rocks and pulling himself along. He stopped at Frank's feet, and when he looked up, his eyes shone like ebony.

"You can't stop us." It was Booth's voice again, this time wracked with pain and strangled with suffering. "We'll keep coming back, keep fomenting strife and war and death, until our boss has what he wants. Until he's running the ranch. Tell the Boss-man that, when you get back to Hell."

The fire intensified and the policeman cried out one last time as his body turned to ash and blew away on the cold winter wind. Snowflakes swirled across the cobblestones, as if sweeping up all evidence the man had ever been there.

Spike, Camille, and Stan had moved on the remaining conspirators by the time Frank tore his gaze from the spot where Booth had been destroyed. They held the remaining gangsters hostage, rifles trained on them.

"What do we do with these ones, Marshal?" Spike jabbed the barrel of his rifle at the closest policeman.

"No choice. We gotta send those souls back to Hell." Without waiting for a reply, Frank strode toward the church. No sooner had he pushed through the door than shots rang out from the street. A moment later, more shots, and Frank knew the Booth gang had all be returned to their eternal prison.

Inside, he found the few remaining parishioners helping the president and Curtis down from the crosses. The instant Curtis saw him, the boy broke into a run, crashed into Frank, and threw his arms around his waist.

"Thank you." His sobs muffled themselves into Frank's heavy duster.

Frank winced as pain rifled from his shoulder down into his arm.

Benjamin Harrison looked Frank and his friends over from top to bottom, then shook his head.

"I don't rightly know what just happened, but I owe you a debt of gratitude, Mister..."

"Butcher, Mr. President. Frank Butcher."

"And you're a federal marshal?"

Frank hesitated. "Not exactly, sir. It's...difficult to explain."

Curtis hadn't yet let go of Frank, his fingers clawed into the duster's coarse fabric.

"Well, Mr. Butcher, I'd like to honor you with a banquet at the White House."

Frank raised a gloved hand. "I wouldn't do that, Mr. President. What happened here today, I wouldn't suggest telling anyone."

Stan entered and stood beside Frank. "I think I got most of the people who were outside." His eyes glowed blue, and the president took a step back.

"Don't worry, Mr. President," Frank said. "Stan here's just making sure this doesn't become an issue later. He's gonna help you relax a bit."

Stan's fingers danced in a series of moves Frank wasn't sure he could have imitated. A blue glow engulfed his hand, and he reached out to put his finger between the president's eyes.

President Harrison rocked a bit on his feet, Frank catching his forearm and guiding him to a pew. The president sat and closed his eyes.

"He'll sleep for a few minutes," Stan said. "We should go, before he wakes up and asks too many questions."

Frank nodded and moved to the door, the boy still latched to his side. Once they were outside, their breath fogging the air in front of them, Camille led them to a back alley, where they gathered and huddled close.

"Looks like you two got what you wanted," Frank pointed to Camille and Spike. "You got through this one without dying. You get to stay here for a while."

The grin that bent Camille's lips upward sent a chill down Frank's backbone. He was glad to not be her unfinished business.

"What about you, Marshal?" Spike put a beefy hand

on Frank's shoulder. "You gonna stay on with us here?"

Frank shook his head. "That wasn't my deal with the judges. I gotta go back. Besides, after this, I got some atonin' to do."

Curtis detached himself from Frank's side and glared up at him.

"I'm sorry, son." Frank's heart broke in two. "If I could stay with you, I would, but them ain't the rules. Besides, it looks like I have some work to do back in the eternal fires."

Camille's eyes narrowed. "Stay out of it, Frank. There could be forces in play stronger than you can handle."

Frank shrugged and smiled at her. "I'm already involved, according to Mills. Can't get out, so I might as well try to fight."

Even Stan looked like he'd swallowed something sour. Curtis turned his back and walked a few feet away.

"Go then. I'll be here when you get back. Or not."

And with that, he stalked away into the drifting snow. Stan moved silently to Frank's side.

"When I'm gone," Frank told him, "wipe him, too."

"He'll forget what you said. He'll forget you saved him."

Frank sighed and nodded. "You suppose these are all the weapons the gang had?"

Stan shrugged. "Likely not. I suspect they have some rebels around, still armed and waiting for a signal that won't come now."

"Then, I suppose we did our jobs."

Stan nodded and followed Curtis into the night.

"You need help going back to Hell this time?" He hadn't heard Camille come up behind him and kicked himself for being careless. "I could pull the trigger for you."

Frank chuckled and faced the hooker. Her blonde curls tumbled out from under her floppy hat, and she played with the Bowie in her hands.

"Don't go gettin' yourself killed finishing up your business here." He wiped a snowflake from her cheek, but she fended off his fingers with a gentle brush of her blade. "And don't get Spike killed."

She laughed at that, kissed her fingers, and pressed them against his cheek.

"Be careful in Hell. No one there is trustworthy, especially not those judges."

She strolled off into the darkness, too. Frank turned and walked up to Spike as the big bartender loaded shells into his shotgun.

"Think I might borrow that piece?" Frank said. "Time for me to go back."

Spike rolled his eyes. "I suppose I can get another. Just make sure you take out the green shell."

Frank nodded, clapped Spike on the shoulder, and wandered deeper into the alley.

CHAPTER SIXTEEN

Frank stood, fists clenched at his sides, glaring at the silhouettes of the judges as they loomed in front of the burning wall in their chambers. All three returned his glare, pairs of blue, green, and hateful red eyes carving through his soul.

"You managed to create even more noise than you did last time, Marshal." Earp spoke for the other two, his voice full of sand and fire. "Deflecting the Boss-man's attention was much harder for us this time.

"Not only did you make noise, you killed even more innocents than you did last time, and by my count, that included one child!"

Frank's fingernails dug into his palms, warm blood running down between his knuckles. His patience was worn thin, and he'd had enough of answering for that particular sin. But he held his tongue, for snapping at these three would only make things worse for him.

Webber growled, his red eyes flaring, hand twitching near the hellish six-shooter on his hip.

"We told you to keep it quiet, Marshal. Did you not understand that part of our instructions? Or did you just not care—"

Frank's temper snapped. "You knew I'd do a lot of killin'. It's what I do. Were you three going to tell me about the cambions, or was that little detail left out on purpose?"

That silenced Webber, and the judge leaned back, his eyes fading to a seething crimson.

Hickok twisted one end of his moustache. "We didn't know about the cambions. They were slipped out of Hell without our knowledge."

Frank wondered if the marshal was showing his poker tell by fiddling with his moustache, but decided it didn't matter. The judges lied all the time anyway.

"You know what it means, just as well as I do. Booth wasn't strong enough to call those beasts out on his own. He had help from the inside."

The judges conferred, their heads leaning close, voices like serpents' hisses, until they spoke as one. "It is not possible. The help must have come from a living person. A witch, most likely."

"That's hogwash, and you know it."

Frank winced, expecting an explosion of pain in his head, but none came.

"What makes you say so, Marshal?" Earp leaned forward.

"Let's just say I have it from a reliable source."

"You mean that self-righteous servant of the Honcho, Mills?"

Frank remained silent, so Webber spoke.

"Yes, let's talk about that angel-friend of yours. Your interaction with someone from the other kingdom makes us question your loyalty to Hell and the Boss-man. For all we know, you could now be a rebel, sent to undermine the Boss-man's rule in Hell. Maybe we should destroy you where you stand."

Frank narrowed his eyes. "I thought you three worked for both...bosses. Why you so interested in protecting one over the other?"

"The boss of that other kingdom ain't here." Earp's voice was matter-of-fact, like this was common knowledge. "We see the Boss-man all the time, but that honcho...never. He don't care one whit for us."

Another mental note Frank tucked away for future use.

"We should punish him." Webber's eyes narrowed to crimson gashes. "Less time in the pit, and more spent in his cell, re-living his son's death. He made a mess of this mission."

Frank fought back a hasty reply, then sighed. He was Hell's Butcher, a killer. He deserved whatever they threw at him.

"What did the angel tell you, Marshal?" Hickok glanced sidelong at Webber.

Frank thought about lying, but they'd know as soon as he did. And they'd torture it out of him anyway.

"He said Hell has a rebel problem. Said one of you was playing with me for their own ends, and that things in Hell were going south in a hurry."

"Lies!" Webber shot from his chair, nearly knocking the table over. The other judges looked at him with something akin to confusion. "We'll hear no more of this fallen angel's lies."

Frank's temper got the better of him. "Then, maybe I should tell them all to the Boss-man himself and see what he thinks of your malarkey!"

Webber's hand shot forward, fingers pointed at Frank's head, and in a heartbeat, it felt like someone had jabbed an icepick between his eyes. Frank cried out and fell to his knees, then his back. He clawed at his face, trying to pull the knife from his skull, but finding only his own skin there.

His vision blurred, and darkness closed in from all sides. He felt not only his consciousness, but his very life draining from him, his very existence. Webber was destroying his soul, doing what the green bullet would have done, only slowly. Torturously.

"Let him up."

Frank recognized Earp's voice above the pain echoing through his mind. Still the pain burned on.

"Webber, we need him. The Boss-man needs him."

Slowly, the pain melted away, leaving Frank broken and heaving for air on his hands and knees. He couldn't even muster the strength to lift his head, but he could feel Webber's glare burning a hole in him still.

"Know your place, Frank Butcher." Webber's voice was icy calm now, frigid as death itself. "You're Hell's Marshal, and your job is bringing back the souls we charge you with. Don't start thinkin' you're any more than that."

Frank felt rather than saw or heard Webber leave the room. He looked up in time to see the other two following him out. Earp stopped and looked over his shoulder.

"Wars happen in Hell all the time, Marshal. Webber's right—stay out of it, if you know what's good for you."

And with that, he exited the room, leaving Frank on his knees until Damon came to get him. As the jailer led him back to his cell, Frank wondered if he hadn't just put his foot in a giant bear trap.

www.ingramcontent.com/pod-product-compliance
Lightning Source LLC
Chambersburg PA
CBHW070927130626
46555CB00001B/313